"What a view," came the rich voice from behind her.

Elizabeth grinned and turned away from her perusal of the refrigerator's contents. Even first thing in the morning, Ron Powers was a vision. He was all man—from his rugged, well-toned physique to his no-nonsense, take-charge persona.

"You're not too bad to look at yourself."

He stretched, and the hard muscles of his stomach rippled. LL Cool J didn't have nothing on her man. Ron strolled over to her.

"And what, may I ask, are you doing?" As he spoke, he took the carton of eggs out of her hand and set it on the countertop.

"I was starting breakfast. After last night *and* this morning, I'm starved."

"But what is today?" he asked, like a teacher quizzing a student.

She frowned for a moment in confusion. "Uh, Tuesday."

"That's the wrong answer. Today is your day off, Elizabeth. It's time that you let me take care of *you* for a change."

"Well, since you put it that way." She tiptoed over and kissed his soft lips.

Books by Donna Hill

Kimani Romance

Love Becomes Her
Saving All My Lovin'
If I Were Your Woman
After Dark

DONNA HILL

began her career in 1987. She now has more than fifty published titles to her credit. Three of her novels have been adapted for television. She has been featured in *Essence,* the New York *Daily News, USA TODAY, Today's Black Woman* and *Black Enterprise,* among many others. She has appeared on numerous radio and television stations across the country, and her work has appeared on several bestseller lists, including *Essence, Emerge* and *The Dallas Morning News,* among others. She has received numerous awards for her body of work, including a career achievement award, and she was the first recipient of the Trailblazer Award. She's also received commendations for her community service. Donna cowrote the screenplay for *Fire,* which enjoyed limited theater release before going to DVD. As an editor she has packaged several highly successful novels, two of which were nominated for awards. She organizes author-centered events and workshops through her editorial and promotions company, Donna Hill Promotions, and provides publicity and marketing services for authors. She is also a writing instructor at the Frederick Douglass Creative Arts Center in New York. Donna currently writes full-time and lives in Brooklyn with her family. You may contact her via her Web site at www.donnahill.com. Donna is represented by the Steele-Perkins Literary Agency.

After Dark

DONNA HILL

KIMANI
ROMANCE

This series is dedicated to all the mature ladies who are
bringing sexy back! You know who you are.

KIMANI PRESS™

ISBN-13: 978-0-373-86024-1
ISBN-10:   0-373-86024-2

AFTER DARK

Copyright © 2007 by Donna Hill

www.kimanipress.com

Printed in U.S.A.

Dear Reader,

I'm so glad you decided to pick up *After Dark*.
All my other ladies have had a chance to tell their
stories in *Love Becomes Her, Saving All My Lovin'* and
If I Were Your Woman. Now it's Elizabeth's time to shine.
Although she may have been the quiet one of the quartet,
Elizabeth has plenty to say this time out.

Just when Elizabeth thinks she has found the love that
will last her a lifetime, old ghosts from Ron's past come
back to haunt them both. Not to mention that Matt
has realized the error of his ways when he gave up
his wife of twenty-five years, and will do whatever
it takes to win her back.

So hold on to your seat. The *girlz* will definitely be there
for advice and support as they too continue to hold their
own lives and loves together, but it will ultimately be
Elizabeth who must decide which man will capture her
heart for good.

I can't thank you all enough for the support you've
shown this wonderful series. I hope to continue
it with Terri, Dawne and Desiree. Because as you
all know, anything can happen at PAUSE FOR MEN!
So stay tuned.

Happy reading,

Donna

Chapter 1

Ellie reached for her silk robe at the foot of the bed, careful not to disturb Ron as she got up. She slipped the smooth fabric over her naked body and loosely tied the belt. She stood and her muscles ached, but in an all-too-good way.

She smiled to herself as she tiptoed into the kitchen. Her thighs trembled ever so slightly when she walked and she could still feel the fullness of Ron deep inside her—hours later.

In her twenty-five years of marriage, sex had been enjoyable but never mind-blowing. Her ex-husband, Matt, hadn't been particularly adventurous, although, she had to admit, he was caring and always tender. Hmmph, it had all been a facade.

She flipped on the wall switch and her sunny yellow and white kitchen came to life under the muted lighting, courtesy of Ron. His touches were everywhere throughout the two bedroom apartment, from the recessed track lighting, to the mosaic floor tiles, the hand-crafted book case to the refurbished walk-in closet. Even when he wasn't physically with her, his presence was still felt and she loved it.

Elizabeth went into the kitchen to put on a pot of coffee and see what she could throw together for a filling breakfast. She opened the refrigerator and leaned down to scan the shelves.

"What a view," came the rich voice from behind her.

She grinned and turned around. Damn, even first thing in the morning he was a vision to behold.

Ron Powers was all man, from the rugged, well-toned physique to his no-nonsense, take charge persona. Whenever she was with him she knew that he would look after her. At six foot two, with a warm chocolate complexion, a slow sexy smile and bedroom eyes, Ron was not just an appetizer but a full-course meal.

"You're not too bad to look at, yourself. Good morning."

He stretched and the hard muscles of his stomach rippled. LL Cool J didn't have nothing on her man.

He strolled over to her. "And what, may I ask, are you doing?" He took the carton of eggs out of her hand and set them on the white marble countertop.

"I was in the process of starting breakfast. I don't know about you but after last night *and* this morning, I'm starved."

"And what is today?" he asked like a teacher quizzing a student.

She frowned for a moment in confusion. "Um, Tuesday."

"Two points deducted. Today is your day off. That means no work of any kind. I'll take care of breakfast. You work that pretty behind of yours off every day. Let me take care of you for a change."

"Well, since you put it that way…" She tiptoed and kissed his soft lips. "Be my guest. You know where everything is."

"Yep. Go relax—preferably in bed until I'm done."

She gave him a mock salute. "Yes, sir. Is it okay with the sergeant if I take a shower, first?"

"Yes, private, then off to bed with you."

She spun away, undid her belt and let her robe fall to the floor before walking off.

"That kind of behavior will get you the results you're looking for," he called out.

"I hope so," she yelled back.

God she was happy, she thought as the steamy water splashed over her. She used her loofah sponge on her hips and her heels then rubbed her favorite mango and guava shower gel into her skin. Soon the room was immersed in her fragrance. Rinsing off, she reached for her shaver in the shower caddy and touched up under her arms and neatened up her pubic area before a final rinse. She noticed a few gray hairs down there and cringed. Well, looks were deceiving. It may look like it was getting old, but it sure played like a young girl.

She stepped out of the shower and wrapped up in a thick towel before padding off to the adjoining bedroom. No point in getting officially dressed she mused while applying lotion to her body. She had every intention of staying as close to her bed and Ron as possible for the rest of the day. But, at least, she could pretend to clothe herself.

Elizabeth opened her top dresser drawer

where she kept her lingerie. It was filled with lacy undies, garters, thongs in splashes of colors. The kinds of things she'd worn during her marriage, but Matt never seemed to really notice. Ron was a different story. He loved to see her show off her body and always complimented her on the way the dazzling colors looked against her skin. Most of all he enjoyed taking them off of her. She would have thought her basic black or white undergarments would have sufficed until one day they were in the mall and passed a Victoria's Secret store, and Ron insisted that she go in and pick out whatever she wanted.

She was a bit self-conscious at first until she'd felt him next to her and he started making suggestions. She soon discovered what he liked and that she liked it, too. From then on, Ms. Victoria was her best friend.

Elizabeth pulled out a burnt orange demi-pushup bra with a matching thong. She grinned. Ron loved her in orange.

Doing as commanded, she hopped back in bed and turned on the morning news. As usual, it was a litany of chaos: Fires, car accidents, police shootings and terror suspects.

The newscaster's story was on the heightened security measures that the FBI and Homeland

Security were employing to weed out possible suspects here in the States. He went on to say that there was legislation that was being considered allowing the government to tap into the phones of American citizens without a warrant as long as they were considered suspect.

Elizabeth shuddered at the thought. Where would it end? She pointed the remote at the television and began to surf. It was too early in the morning to get depressed. She finally settled on *Monster In-Law* on one of the cable stations. She'd seen it three times, already, but it never failed to make her laugh. The movie was up to the scene where Jennifer Lopez and Jane Fonda have it out at a restaurant.

"Breakfast, as they say, is served, Madame," Ron announced with a really bad British accent. He walked in with a large tray.

Elizabeth flattened out the covers and propped herself regally against the thick pillows.

"Smells delicious."

Ron placed the tray on her lap. Grits with cheese, a western omelet, wheat toast, coffee and an icy cold glass of orange juice.

"Wow." She looked up at him. "This is wonderful.

"Enjoy it."

"Aren't you going to eat?"

"Yep. Be right back."

Shortly he returned with an identical setup and they watched the movie and laughed their way through the meal.

"I'll take these out to the kitchen," Elizabeth offered once they were finished.

"Nope. I will. Stay put." He took their trays and empty plates into the kitchen and put them in the dishwasher.

When he returned to the bedroom, Elizabeth was sitting up with her arms folded tightly across her waist.

"Something wrong?"

"You don't have to fuss over me, Ron. Seriously."

He came over to the bed and sat down, the side sinking with his weight.

"Look, it's not often that I get a chance to do anything for you. I see you working like a fiend every day running the spa. I know it can't be easy. Ellie, even on your days off you have errands to run and loose ends to tie up. Today, I really want it to be a day off for you."

She smiled at him and cupped his chin in her palm. "Thank you. I really do appreciate it. I have been going nonstop since we opened."

"My point exactly."

Elizabeth stretched and wiggled her toes beneath the sheets. "Okay, I surrender."

"Good." He pushed against her hips and she scooted over, making room for him in the bed.

"How did you manage to get the day off today?" she asked, resting her head against his chest.

"I'm the boss, remember?" He chuckled lightly. "I have a few new jobs coming up, but I'm waiting on the contracts to be finalized. I have Ali running things today. The job up on Lenox is almost finished."

Ron was a private contractor with his own small construction firm specializing in rehabbing brownstones, which was how she'd met him. He was the contractor that was hired to renovate the Harlem brownstone that housed the day spa, *Pause for Men,* as well as her apartment that was on the top floor.

"I still can't get over how Ali was the connection to Stephanie's dad. Fate truly brought them together."

"Yeah. If he hadn't been working on that job for me, he might have never met her. When is she coming back from Texas?"

"I don't know, exactly. I'm sure she wants to

spend as much time with her father as she can. But she probably won't stay away too long. She does have her sister to think about."

"Now, that is a sad story. I don't know how Stephanie has been able to deal with seeing her sister like that all these years."

"It can't be easy. But Stephanie is a tough girl. She may have her faults, but she can hold her own."

"All of your friends, Barbara and Ann Marie are pretty amazing women."

"I only surround myself with the best." She looked up at him and winked. "Including men."

"Hmm, now that's what I like to hear."

In the distance, the faint sound of the downstairs doorbell could be heard. The spa was open for business.

Ron had done an excellent job of soundproofing her place as much as possible to keep out the noise from the spa below. When it was full and the music was playing it would have been a bit much up in the apartment. But for the most part the noise was sufficiently muffled.

Ron leaned over to kiss her just as her telephone rang. She wrinkled her nose and leaned over to pick up the phone on the nightstand.

"Hello? Hi, Carmen. Whatsup?" As she lis-

tened she frowned. "Okay, give me five minutes." She hung up the phone. "I need to run
downstairs for a few minutes."

"For what?"

"There's a problem with the registration program. I just need to check it and I'll be right
back, I swear."

Ron gave her a hard stare. "Don't make me
come down there and get you," he grumbled.

"I love you, too." She popped out of bed and
grabbed her navy blue sweatsuit from the closet,
dressed in a flash then darted out.

When she entered the main floor of the spa
from the side entrance, the exclusive locale
for men only was in full swing. It was barely
10:00 a.m. and the café was already filled with
clients. Several men were signing up for mas-
sages, the workout room was in use and small
group of men simply sat and chatted in the
lounge.

Elizabeth smiled in awe. It was still hard to
believe that one night of drunken brilliance between four girlfriends could have spawned such
a successful endeavor.

She hurried over to Carmen who looked totally flustered behind the computer.

"Oh, thank goodness. I'm so sorry to bug you
on your day off, but I didn't know what else to do."

Elizabeth came behind the desk. "No problem. Let me take a look." She hit a few keys and unlocked the registration program. The new screen popped up. "There you go."

"Thanks." She sighed, looking shamefaced.

"Everything else okay?"

"Yes, so far. I'm really sorry to bug you on your day off."

"Don't worry about it." She took a look around. "Looks like we're going to be busy."

"I know," Carmen said with a sigh.

Elizabeth checked the schedule to see who was on duty. Stephanie was out of town, Barbara had to put in a full day at the hospital and Ann Marie was not due in until three o'clock. Although all of the founding members were pretty much off for the day, they'd hired a very reliable staff to cover the three floors and the basement. And, from what Elizabeth could see, everyone had signed in.

"Okay, if there's nothing else, I'm going to head back upstairs."

"Sure. See you tomorrow." She walked back upstairs, checking out the handsome and fit clientele as she went. Hmmph, hmmph, hmmph she thought in amusement. *It was a tough job watching good-looking, half-dressed men all day, but somebody had to do it.*

Ron was in the shower when she returned so, by habit, she started straightening up the bedroom, then the living room. When she heard the shower stop, she hustled back into the bedroom and greeted Ron with a big smile and not much else.

"Now, that's what I like to see," Ron said in appreciation as his eyes rolled up and down her body. He crossed the room with only a towel draped around his waist. He climbed onto the bed and right up on top of her. He wrapped his arm around her waist and pulled her flush against him. Then he leaned down and kissed her long and slow.

She hummed against his mouth, just as the phone rang again. Ron groaned.

Elizabeth held up a finger. "One minute. Hold that pose." She went to the phone, spoke softly for a few minutes before she hung up. She turned to Ron. "I'm sorry. I need to go downstairs again. I'll be right back."

"Ellie…"

"Right back," she said as she grabbed her clothes and headed for the door before he could protest further.

Apparently, there was some confusion with one of the client's massage appointment and he was making quite a stink. When she got downstairs, Drew, the security guard, was standing near the reception desk ready to toss the irate client out at a moment's notice.

"How can I help you, sir?" Elizabeth said, stepping into the fray. "I'm Elizabeth Lewis, the spa manager."

The man whirled toward her and began going on about how he had an appointment, had paid his monthly dues and how he expected to be serviced at his appointed time. He was a busy man, he declared and didn't have time to wait.

"We'll work this all out." Elizabeth stepped behind the desk and took a look at the schedule on the computer. Yes, there was definitely a conflict. Elizabeth looked up. "Mr. Blaine, first, let me apologize for the wait. It was definitely our error. Unfortunately, the masseuse is not free for another half hour and I know you don't want to wait. This is what I'm willing to do. I will return a month's membership fee to your credit card. And I will personally set up your massage appointment, myself, right now for whatever day and time you are free." She raised a brow and waited for his response.

His puffed up chest slowly deflated. "Fine," he grumbled.

Elizabeth went through a few key strokes, made the deduction then conferred with him about his schedule and made his appointment.

"Thank you."

"You're very welcome, Mr. Blaine. We want to make sure that all of our clients are happy and satisfied."

He walked away.

"Oh, Ellie, I am so sorry. I just didn't know what to do."

Elizabeth patted her shoulder. "It's okay. I'm glad I was here. And now I'm gone." She smiled and walked off.

When she returned upstairs, Ron had gotten dressed and was sitting in front of the television in the living room. She inwardly flinched as she walked inside and quietly closed the door behind her. She went to the couch and sat next to him.

"I'm sorry," she said as sweet as she could. "Carmen is relatively new. Some things she just isn't up to speed on."

Ron turned to her, his expression set in hard lines. "Then, she shouldn't be there alone if she can't handle it.

Elizabeth jerked back slightly from the vehemence of his response.

"I'm not telling you how to run your

business— Well, maybe I am. The purpose of hiring and training someone is because you want them to be able to handle the job with or without supervision. What would she have done if you weren't around?"

"But I *was* around. I'm the manager. It's my responsibility—"

"And you have a life."

She huffed and pushed up from the couch. "For twenty-five years I devoted my life to making a home, being a wife to the exclusion of anything I wanted for myself. I didn't know I could do anything other than cook, clean, decorate and be a wife and mother. This spa opened a new world for me. It's given me a confidence I'd lost. It helped me realize that I'm so much more than I had been."

"I understand that. But, at the same time, Ellie, you can't now allow the job to become your new dependent. At some point, you have to find a way to separate yourself from the job."

She averted her gaze. He didn't understand, not really. How could he comprehend how much it all meant to her? The spa is what helped her heal, got her over the hurdle of Matt's betrayal and the ensuing divorce. If she didn't have the responsibilities of running the spa she would have lost her mind.

"Ell, all I'm saying is make time for you so that you can make time for us. That's all I'm saying," he repeated.

She slunk back over to the couch and plopped down next to him. "I'll try," she murmured.

Ron draped his arm around her shoulder and kissed the top of her head.

Yet, even as she agreed and sat curled in the security of his embrace, she was wondering what was going on downstairs and, more importantly, just how much would her love for her job affect her relationship with Ron.

Chapter 2

Matthew Lewis sat in the quiet of his doctor's office on the Eastside of upper Manhattan. He'd gotten the call from his doctor's nurse that it was very important that he come in as soon as possible. When Matthew questioned why, he was informed that, "the doctor would explain everything."

He didn't like the sound of it. He heard the door open behind him. Dr. Chavis walked in.

"Thank you for coming, Matt," he said as he went around the desk and sat down.

"What's this all about? Is it the tests?"

Dr. Chavis opened a folder on his desk. He

paused for several moments before speaking. He looked directly at Matthew. "The test results are not good. We found elevated PSA levels and, in conjunction with the exam, the swelling of the prostate gives me cause for concern."

Matthew felt as if he'd been punched in the gut. All the color drained from his face.

Dr. Chavis held up his hand. "There is some good news. There are a great deal of treatment options, especially for a man of your age who is in reasonably good health."

The doctor's voice drifted off. Matthew no longer heard him. *Cancer.* The doctor hadn't come right out and said it, but it hung in the air like a bad smell. The word sent a chill through him. His father had died of prostate cancer and so had his uncle. It ran in his family and the risk of it killing him, as well, rose exponentially. That much, he did know.

"I want to get you in the hospital as soon as possible and take some more tests. They'll do a biopsy. After we've examined the tissue under a microscope, we'll know best how to proceed."

Matthew started blankly at the doctor. "When do you want me to come in?"

The doctor opened his appointment book. "Tomorrow at noon."

"Tomorrow?" Fear gripped his gut. "So soon?"

"The sooner the better, Matt, I'm sure you know that."

Matthew swallowed over the dry knot in his throat.

"In your medical history you indicated that both your father and your father's brother died of prostate cancer. That is more reason to take care of this as soon as possible. It could be nothing, but we don't want to risk it."

Matthew nodded numbly.

Dr. Chavis wrote some information down on a slip of paper and handed it to Matthew. He then picked up the phone and called the hospital to make an appointment.

"Do you have any questions that I can answer now?"

Matthew slowly shook his head. He stood. "Thank you, Doctor."

"You'll probably want to have someone accompany you to the hospital to bring you home. Although it is an outpatient procedure, you will be given a local anesthesia. And it's always best to have someone for moral support."

"Sure. Thanks," he murmured.

There was no one, he realized as he wandered to his car. For several moments, he sat behind the wheel, unable to move. No one he could call. That hard truth hit him almost as hard as the doctor's assessment. He'd cut off his friends when he got involved with his secretary. He'd lost Elizabeth. His daughters, although still cordial, resented what he'd done to their mother.

Yet, even knowing what he'd done to his wife, he also knew that, above all else, Elizabeth was a caring woman. When they'd had their last talk months earlier and he'd begged for her to take him back, he'd seen the wavering in her eyes and body, but her pride had won out.

He needed to be with someone right now and the only person he wanted to be with was Ellie.

"I'm going to run down to the supermarket to pick up some things for dinner," Ron said. "I thought I'd whip up my famous veal cutlet parmesan for us."

Elizabeth rubbed her hands together in glee. "Yum. Want me to go with you?"

"Naw. It's starting to rain, anyway. I'll be back in flash."

"I'll fix a salad and prepare some pasta with that fancy pasta maker you got me." She winked.

"Can't keep a busy woman down," he joked, then walked over to her. He lifted her chin with the tip of his finger. "Listen, about earlier, I know the spa is important to you. I know they depend on you, a little too much in my opinion, but I understand. All I was saying was that I worry about you and I don't want you to burn yourself out with everyone else's issues. You spent the better part of your life doing that. It should be Ellie time now." He shrugged and gave her a crooked grin. "Forgive me if I sounded like a chauvinist pig."

"Hmm, let me mull that over. I'll forgive you on one condition." She planted her hands on her hips.

He frowned. "What condition?"

"That the veal melts in my mouth." She gave him a wicked grin and giggled.

"Lady, you're on!" He kissed the bridge of her nose and hurried out.

"Take the umbrella by the door," she called out.

As she hummed her way to kitchen, she really took Ron's comments to heart. She'd initially been stung by his proprietary tone but she did understand that his concern stemmed from his feelings for her. He'd been her number-one supporter when she'd told him that, of the four women, she felt best about taking over the daily management of the spa. Neither of them had

imagined that it would require all of her time.
And the fact that she lived right above hadn't
made it any easier.

The first thing on her agenda when she returned to work was to bring everyone up to speed
about what to do when she was unavailable, like
on her day off.

She took out some mixed greens for the salad,
a red onion, some mushrooms and baby tomatoes. She began washing them in the colander
just as the phone rang.

Wiping her hands on a dishtowel, she picked
up the phone in the kitchen.

"Ellie, I'm really sorry to bother you again."

"Whatever it is, Carmen, I know you can handle it," she said cutting her off at the pass. "If not,
it will have to wait until tomorrow."

"I wish it could wait. Marva, the part-time
therapist, is here. She needs to pick up her check
but it's locked in the safe."

Elizabeth groaned. Unfortunately she had no
choice. The combination to the safe was only
known by the owners. Well, if she hurried, she
could dart downstairs and get back up before
Ron returned. "I'll be right there."

She rushed onto the main floor of the spa and
went to the office downstairs, opened the safe

and got the check, then hurried upstairs. Marva was standing there waiting.

"Thanks so much, Ellie," she said, taking the check. "How's your day off going?" she asked innocently.

"It's going."

"Well, good night." Marva walked off.

"Oh, Elizabeth, before I forget—"

"No more emergencies."

"No, it's nothing like that. You got a phone call, earlier."

"Did you take a message?"

"Yes, but he said it was urgent that you call as soon as possible. He wanted me to give him your home phone number, but I said I couldn't do that."

"Who was it?"

"Matthew Lewis. He said he was your husband."

Her heart knocked. *Ex,* she thought but didn't say it. "What did he want?"

"He said that it was an emergency and to please call him." She handed her the neat message from the pad. All the items on the preprinted pink slip had been checked off: Date, time, name of caller and degree of importance— *Urgent.*

Elizabeth took the pink paper, thanked Carmen and went back up to her apartment. She stared at the digits. What did Matthew want and what could be so important?

Matthew had put her through hell and back. His affair had rocked her to the core and it still stung whenever she thought about it. And it wasn't so much that he'd had an affair, but how he told her about it. He had wanted to buy her out of the house so that he could move into it with his mistress.

Her stomach churned just thinking about it. She put the number in the drawer next to the sink. Out of sight, out of mind. Whatever it was, he'd have to figure out how to deal with it himself—just like everyone else!

By the time she'd finished with the salad and prepared her special dressing, Ron was walking through the door.

"Honey, I'm home," he sang out.

Elizabeth smiled. She liked the sound of that.

They spent the rest of the evening, working, laughing and talking side by side.

"So, am I forgiven?" Ron asked as they cleaned up after dinner.

"I need to make deals like that all the time," she said, rubbing her stomach and running her tongue across her lips.

"I take that as a yes." He took a napkin and wiped the corner of her mouth.

"And you would be right." She kissed him quickly on the lips. "How 'bout a movie?"

"Sounds good. I can finish up in here. You go pick something."

"Drama, comedy, thriller?"

"Hmm, thriller. That way, when you get scared you can leap right into my arms." He winked.

She shook her head and chuckled. "I'll see what I can do." She went off to the living room.

Ron finished rinsing the dishes and stacking them in the dishwasher, took the clean dishes out of the draining board and put them in the overhead cabinet. Then the silverware. He opened the drawer and quickly realized it was the wrong one. He started to close it but reached for the piece of paper inside. It was one of the spa's message sheets, complete with the *Pause for Men* logo.

That wasn't what stopped him. It was the date— *Today*. And it was a message from her ex-husband. Reflexively, his jaw clenched and his mind immediately recapped his first impromptu meeting with Matthew Lewis. He and Ellie had been out all Sunday afternoon and had decided to stop at an outdoor café, when Matthew'd walked up on them. They'd exchanged some heated words and it had nearly turned physical.

He was the one who'd comforted Elizabeth when she was going through the pain and stress of her divorce, the sale of her house. He helped her feel strong enough to live alone for the first time in her adult life. And all of that was because Matthew Lewis had wanted someone younger. It had taken more than six months for Elizabeth to really feel good about herself, begin to open up to him and live life again. What the hell could Matthew Lewis want with her now? More importantly, why didn't Elizabeth tell him that he'd called?

Ron held the slip of paper in his hand, debating whether to ask her about it or to see if she would tell him on her own. He opted for the latter and put the paper back in the drawer.

He took one last look around the kitchen, turned out the lights and joined Elizabeth on the couch.

After the movie, Ron yawned and stretched. It was almost nine o'clock. Either he was going to stay the night or he needed to be heading home. But he knew, if he stayed and Ellie didn't mention the call from her husband, it would eat him up all night. And, if he went home, he knew he'd really let his mind go on a free-for-all.

He angled his body on the couch. "Ell, when

I was in the kitchen I was putting some of the silverware away and pulled open the wrong drawer.
I saw the note from Matt."

Her eyes widened for an instant in surprise.
"Oh."

He waited to see if she would elaborate. She
didn't. "Have you called him back?"

"No." She folded her arms in front of her and
Ron knew it was her way of saying she didn't
want to discuss it.

He reached over and unloosened her arms.
"Do you plan to?"

She snapped her head in his direction. "I don't
know. And that's my honest and final answer."

Ron drew in a long breath. "Fair enough." He
pushed up from the couch. "I'm going to head
on home. Busy day tomorrow."

She reached up and took his hand. "Is that the
real reason?"

"What other reason could there be?"

"That you're upset about Matthew calling me."

"That's part of it. I just remember everything
he put you through, Ell. I thought he was out of
your life, and ours, for good."

"He is."

"Apparently, he doesn't think so. Maybe you
should call him."

She glanced away.

Ron leaned down and kissed her lightly. "I'll give you a call tomorrow. Rest well."

Elizabeth started to stop him from leaving, but didn't. She watched him walk out. The truth was she needed some time to herself. Since she'd gotten the note from Matt, as much as she tried to push it to the back of her mind, it kept running to the front of the line.

She prepared for bed but spent most of the night at war with her emotions.

The following morning, Elizabeth was up and out. If she'd slept a solid two hours she would be surprised. She went down to the spa and began her daily ritual of turning off the alarms, checking the stock and booting up the computers.

She checked the staff roster and was happy and relieved to see that her best friend, Barbara, would be arriving for the morning shift. Some words of wisdom from Barbara was just the thing she needed.

The staff soon began to arrive and *Pause for Men* was open for business. It never ceased to amaze Elizabeth how many well-to-do men had so much free time in the middle of the day. Barbara breezed in, all smiles and full of energy.

"You sure look happy," Elizabeth greeted as

Barbara tucked her knapsack beneath the registration desk.

"Life is good and Wil is even better." She flashed a wicked wink.

Everyone thought that, Michael, Barbara's young NBA star boyfriend turned ex-fiancé, had put a pep in Barbara's step, but there was no doubt that Wil was the fuel that fired up her tank.

"How are you doing?" Barbara asked, still beaming.

"Not bad. Sort of had a day off yesterday."

"What do you mean, 'sort of'?"

Elizabeth recapped her interrupted day.

"Girl, you need to turn off your phone when you're off. Period." She planted her hand on her hip. "How long has Carmen been here?"

"A couple of months."

"She should know how to run this place on her own, by now. That's why we hired her."

"Same thing Ron said."

"I take it he didn't appreciate the interruptions."

"That's an understatement." She paused. "I need to run something by you."

"Sure." Barbara hopped up on the stool.

Elizabeth told Barbara about the message from Matt.

"Wow. Well, did you call him back?"

"No. Ron found the note."

"Ouch. What did he say?"

"He wanted to know the same thing you did and why Matt would have the nerve to call me after everything he put me through. To make a long story short, he didn't spend the night."

"You need to handle it. And you need to ask yourself why you will or won't call Matt back. It could be anything."

"Or it could just be another of his ploys to get me back."

"Would that bother you? I mean, you're in love with Ron, right? He asked you to marry him. It's over with you and Matt so it shouldn't matter. Right?"

"Right." She looked at her bare hand. The ring was coming, she told herself.

"So, what's the problem?"

Elizabeth sighed. "Twenty-five years is a long time. We shared a lot, good and bad."

Barbara's voice softened. "Do you still have feelings for Matt?"

"When I push all the anger and hurt out of the way…I remember, ya know?"

Barbara squeezed her shoulder. "Then call him and set your mind and your feelings to rest."

She looked at Barbara with a soft smile. "Thanks. I think I will."

"Good. Now, in the meantime, let's see how we can assist some of these fine-ass men up in here."

They both giggled and began their day.

Chapter 3

Agent Brian Jennings sat in front of his computer in his cramped office, scanning the list of names and affiliations that had been added to the "watch list." He felt really uncomfortable spying on U.S. citizens but, according to Homeland Security, there were just as many threats from within as from without.

Jennings's job was to trace all activists, dating as far back as the sixties, from a dizzying array of groups and to see if any names matched current residents of New York City.

This whole operation brought to his mind the dark stories of the Hoover and McCarthy era, where citizens were targeted, blacklisted, harassed, jailed and spied on. Careers and lives were ruined. The country was demoralized. It was an ugly time in American history and it appeared that those times were being revisited.

The screen flashed "Match." He clicked on the icon and a picture and all relevant data appeared on the screen.

Ronald Powers, age 56, West 132nd Street, former Black Panther member, Atlanta Georgia. Owner of Powers Construction.

Brian went over all of the information, including Powers's arrest record during a melee on Grove Street in Atlanta. He'd been clean ever since. However, he was now involved in construction and had access to shipments and, from what was on the screen, his shipments of materials came from a supplier in Philadelphia. That supplier was already on the watch list because of his relations in the Middle East.

"Damn," Brian murmured. He printed out the data. He'd have to turn the information over to his supervisor. As much as Brian figured there was nothing to it but coincidence, Special Agent Luke Hargrove—better known as Hard-ass—wouldn't feel the same way. He'd want Brian to dig until he reached China.

Reluctantly, he put the info together for the meeting that was scheduled in the next ten minutes. He'd be expected to make a presentation.

"Hey, Brian, how's it going?" Adam Collins, his sometimes partner, asked.

Brian barely looked up. He'd been saddled with Adam for the past two months. And, to say that Adam was a stickler for the rule book was an understatement. If one were to look up *brown nose* in the dictionary, Adam's picture would be right under the definition.

"Meeting in a few minutes," Brian muttered.

Adam leaned down, lowering his voice. "Hey, how's your list coming?"

Brian lifted his head to look into inquiring blue eyes. "Fine." He picked up his folder and tucked it under his arm. He made show of checking his watch. "Gonna be late." He headed off.

Luke Hargrove stood at the head of the long conference table with the projection screen behind him. Show and tell, Brian thought as he took a seat.

Hargrove got straight to the point of the meeting: Building the database of possible suspects for investigation. Each of the agents had a different territory to cover. The different areas were displayed on a large screen at the front of the room. Hargrove had the agents go around the table and detail the information they'd gathered, no matter how minute. Finally, it was Brian's turn.

"I've only come up with one lead that is even close to being worthwhile." He detailed the information he had gathered on Ron Powers.

Luke glared at him the entire time he spoke. "You don't sound as if you think there is anything to this," Luke said.

"It's so circumstantial—"

"Verdicts have been built and won on circumstances, Agent Jennings. It's not up to you to decide. It's your duty to follow up on each and every lead, even when *you* don't feel it's credible," he said. "Do I make myself clear?"

"Yes, sir."

Hargrove looked around the room. "If there's nothing else…"

The assembled agents looked at each other wanting nothing more than to get out of the room and away from the presence of Hargrove.

They silently dared each other to make a question or a comment.

"Meeting adjourned."

The agents filed out. Before Brian could scurry back to his office, Adam caught up with him.

"The info you gave Hargrove sounds pretty credible to me. We need to get on it."

Brian cut him a look. The quicker they got this over with, the quicker he could move on to something that didn't turn his stomach. "Yeah, first thing in the a.m., we'll pay Mr. Powers a visit."

If he didn't know better, he'd swear that Adam was licking his chops.

Ron was slow getting himself together the following morning. Normally, he wasn't a possessive or jealous guy. Most of the women he'd known and had been involved with had never reached a level where it'd mattered much what they did. Relationships weren't something that he'd been especially good at. He'd been accused of being cold, distant, a nonparticipant by one woman. Dee Martin was about as close as he'd come to having anything real. She'd lasted longer than most. The more he'd tried to push her away, the tighter she'd held on, until, one day, she just gave up and walked out of his life. That was more than fifteen years ago. After Dee, it was a stream of casual affairs. No one could put up with his lack of emotion.

But then he met Elizabeth and something inside of him woke up. It wasn't dark inside, anymore. He pulled on his work shirt and tucked it into his jeans. Maybe he was trying too hard to make up for lost time and maybe he should back off and give her some space to work out whatever it was she felt for her ex. He grabbed his backpack and headed out.

When he arrived at his storefront office, Ali was already there.

"Hey, man. How was your day off with lady love?"

Ron mumbled something incoherent.

"That good, huh?"

Ron tossed his bag on the table, went to the coffeepot and poured himself a cup. He drank it black and hot.

Ali looked at him with a frown. "What's up? You all right?"

Ron blew out a breath and sat down on the edge of the weather-beaten wood desk.

Ron and Ali went way back as friends, having met each other in Atlanta years before. Ali was known as Melvin back then and, for some reason, he and Ron had connected. They'd pro-

After Dark

tested together, marched together and bonded in a way Ron had not experienced before. When you got down to it, Ali was the only real male friend that Ron had and could trust.

"It's Ellie."

"What about her? She isn't sick, is she?"

He shook his head. "No, nothing like that."

"So, what is it?" Ali leaned against the wall and waited.

Ron told him about finding the note and Ellie's response.

"Man, you gotta remember, she was married to the man for twenty-five years. No matter what kinda mess he might have put her through, that's a lot of time and they have kids together."

"I know all of that—" he tapped his temple with his finger "—in my head."

"Hey, from what I can see, Ellie really digs you, man. And I know you care about her or you wouldn't have asked her to marry you. And that's something I never thought would happen." He laughed lightly. "Let her work it out. It'll be all right. I can't see her going back to him, if that's what you're worried about."

Ron looked up at Ali. "It has happened, you know."

"Yeah, on TV." He chuckled again. "You need

to relax. Your problem my good brother is that you ain't really been in love before. It will truly mess with your natural mind."

"What if he wants her back?"

"He probably does. What man wouldn't? But that's not your issue. You stay on your game and, however it plays out, that's what's gonna happen. Simple as that." He moved toward the coffeepot. "When are you gonna get that woman a ring, anyway? Asking her is just a place holder."

Ron snickered. "Yeah. Well, I'm working on it. I want it to be something special, ya know?"

"Don't wait too long." He glanced toward the door. "Looks like we got company, the suit-and-tie kind."

Chapter 4

She'd debated enough. The longer she put it off, the longer she wouldn't be able to concentrate. She went downstairs to the office for some privacy and closed the door behind her. For a few minutes, she stared at the phone then finally gave in, picked it up and dialed Matt's number.

He answered on the second ring.

"It's Ellie. You left me a message to call you."

"Thank you," he began.

She came around the desk and sat down. "What did you want, Matthew?"

"I know I have no right to ask you anything…"

That's an understatement, she thought.

"But, I—I need you."

"What! Look, I don't have time for this—"

"I'm sick, Ellie," he said, cutting her off.

She flinched. "Sick? What do you mean?"

"I'm going in for a biopsy this morning."

Her heart started to race. "A biopsy for what?"

He explained what the doctor'd told him, and she grew more alarmed by the moment. She knew his family history and what the risks were for him.

"Matt...I don't... I'm sorry."

"I don't have anyone else, Ellie. The doc said I should have someone there after the... procedure. I was hoping that you would come."

Her emotions and her thoughts got all tangled together until she couldn't separate one from the other. The emotional Ellie was ready to come to the rescue, as always. The rational Ellie, the one who'd been hurt and demoralized, had her feet stuck in cement.

"What hospital?" she finally asked.

"Sloane Kettering."

Her eyes squeezed shut at the sound of the name. It was a world-renowned cancer-treatment center. "I... What time do you have to be there?"

"Eleven. I was getting ready to leave when you called."

She thought about her responsibilities at the spa. But Barbara was there and Ann Marie was due to arrive midday. They could hold things down along with the rest of the staff.

"All right. I'll be there as soon as I can."

"Thank you, Ellie," he said, and it sounded to her as if his voice was breaking. "I really appreciate it."

"I'll see you soon." She hung up the phone.

She had a sick, sinking sensation in the pit of her stomach. She'd wished a lot of things on her ex-husband. She'd wished that he would suffer and be hurt as much as she had. She'd devoted her life to him and their twin daughters and then, without warning, she'd been tossed to the curb like old shoes. She'd become a statistic, a cliché. Wife tossed aside for young secretary. How pitiful was that?

It had taken her months, and the support of Barbara, Stephanie and Ann Marie, to get her through the day-to-day without falling apart. Then she met Ron and took a big chance by allowing him into her life and her heart. But she did, and hadn't regretted a moment.

Yet, she hadn't told Ron about Matt's call and the question of "why not?" had plagued her all night long. Maybe there was no easy answer, she concluded as she finally got to her feet. But a hidden part of her knew that it wasn't that simple.

Barbara was at the front desk when Ellie came back upstairs.

"There you are. I was getting ready to go down to the massage room. My first client will be here—" She took a good look at Elizabeth's strained expression. "What's wrong?"

"I just got off the phone with Matt."

"And?"

"He's going in the hospital for a biopsy. They think it might be cancer."

"Oh, Ellie. I'm so sorry. How is he? I mean, mentally?"

"Scared. I could tell by his voice." She looked at Barbara. "I've never heard him sound like that before, not in all the years of our marriage."

"Of course he's scared. Who wouldn't be? Wow, I don't know what to say."

"He wants me to come to the hospital. I told him I would."

Barbara nodded. "How do you really feel about that?"

"Conflicted. But I said I would, so I'm going."

"Sure. We can handle things around here."

"What if…"

"Don't even go there. You don't know for sure."

"Maybe I should call the girls."

"Why don't you wait until you know something more definite. They'll only worry."

"You're right." She looked around, momentarily off balance. "I better get going."

Barbara reached out and wrapped her in a hug. "It's going to be all right, whatever happens, and you know we're here for you, girl."

She sniffed, suddenly feeling weepy. "Thanks."

By the time she arrived at the hospital and found a parking space she was a nervous wreck. Maybe she should have called her daughters; at least, then someone would be there with her. She went through the main entrance and asked for directions to oncology at the information desk.

The ride up the elevator seemed to last forever. Finally, the doors slid open onto the floor. She looked left then right for the nursing station, then walked toward it.

"Excuse me. I'm Mrs. Lewis. My…husband is here for a biopsy."

The nurse looked at her chart then smiled

benignly up at Elizabeth. "Yes, he's just gone in. It will be a little while. We have a lounge down the hall to your left. You can wait there if you wish and someone will come and get you when your husband is brought to recovery."

"Thank you." She felt light-headed, as if she was walking through someone else's reality. The hum of machines and the squish of thick-soled shoes, the clanging of metal carts all gave her a chill that went straight to her bones. Room after room was lined up with patients under various levels of care. Any one of them could be Matt.

Her stomach knotted. She had to think positively. The test would come back, everything would be fine and it would all be a big mistake. She found the lounge and took a seat in the far corner by the window, away from several others who sat vigil. She held on to her positive thoughts like a life raft for the next two hours. Then it was snatched out of her grip.

"Mrs. Lewis?"

The sick sensation rushed to her throat. She gripped her purse to her chest. "Yes."

The doctor came forward. He extended his hand. She thought she shook it but she couldn't be sure.

"I'm Dr. Chavis. Why don't we go down to my office where we can talk in private."

"Is Matthew all right?" she asked as he led her out.

"The biopsy went fine. But let's talk in my office."

He opened the door to a small, cramped space. "Sorry about the mess." The desk was loaded with file folders. "Please have a seat."

Elizabeth sat down.

"I'll get right to the point, Mrs. Lewis, because there is never an easy way to put this. Your husband has cancer."

The room shifted for a moment.

"But we believe we caught it early enough. He has several treatment options…"

He went on to explain the various procedures, from freezing the cells, to implanting radiation seeds to surgery.

She listened and wasn't listening at the same time. The Matt she saw in her head was the handsome knight who'd stood at the end of the aisle and had said "I Do." He was the man who'd given her two beautiful, perfect girls, who'd worked hard to build a life and home for his family. He was the man she'd loved first and, she'd thought always, from the bottom of her heart. Matt was vibrant, healthy, strong and determined. That's the man she saw in her mind.

"He's going to need a lot of support during treatment, no matter what option he chooses," the doctor was saying.

Elizabeth focused on Dr. Chavis. The man the doctor was describing wasn't the man she knew, but she also understood that she would get to know this Matt, as well. She nodded her head. "What now?" she was finally able to say.

"The two of you need to talk about what you want to do. And come to a decision as soon as possible. The earlier we get his treatment started, the better his chances will be."

"Can I see him now?"

"I'll take you to the recovery room."

When she walked into the room, Matt was on the bed with his eyes closed. Her heart jumped. She slowly approached.

He turned his head and opened his eyes. A look of relief washed over his face. "Hi."

She came to the rail of the bed. "Hi. How are you feeling?"

"Tired. But okay, I guess. I have to wait about an hour and then I can go home."

Elizabeth nodded. "I spoke with Dr. Chavis."

"So he, uh, told you everything?"

"Yes. Matt, I'm so sorry."

He drew in a breath. "Yeah, me, too." He forced a laugh. "Life, huh?"

She was quiet, and looked around, not wanting him to see the fear in her eyes. He reached for her hand.

"Thank you for coming, Ell, really."

"I told you I would."

"I know, and you didn't have to, but that's the kind of woman you are."

"Matt…don't."

He turned away and looked up at the ceiling. "I made some mistakes, Ell."

She pressed her lips together. She didn't want to hear this.

"I messed up, with you, the girls, everything. I got to thinking that maybe this was my punishment for hurting you."

"Matt—"

"Just hear me out. I know I have no right to ask you anything, but I need you, Ell. Really need you. I know I can't get through this alone."

Oh, how their roles had reversed, she thought. For years it had been her who'd depended on Matthew. Depended on him for everything, from finances to happiness. When he pulled the rug out from under her, she'd felt as if she'd been dropped into a bottomless pit and would never stop falling. Now it was Matt who needed her and she wasn't sure how to handle that.

"The doctor said you need to make some decisions about…your treatment as soon as possible."

"I was hoping that we could do that together."

"This is your life, Matt. Your decision."

"It's *our* life. We may not be legally bound together, any longer, but you'll always be my wife, Ell. Always."

She couldn't do this. She couldn't let him manipulate her emotions like this.

She lifted her chin. "Did you drive?"

"I took a car service."

"I'll be in the waiting room. Have the nurse or someone come and get me when you're ready. I'll take you home." She turned and walked out before he had a chance to say anything else. But, instead of going to the lounge, she went to the ladies' room, found an empty stall and wept.

Chapter 5

Ron got up from the edge of the desk as the two men came through the door. He knew who they were before they opened their mouths. They all looked the same, so inconspicuous that you'd have to be blind not to see they were government men.

"Can I help you?" Ron asked.

The first man took off his prerequisite sunglasses. "I'm Agent Jennings and this is Agent Collins."

Ali came to stand next to Ron. "You guys are pretty far away from home." He folded his arms across his broad chest.

"Local business. We're looking for Ron Powers." Agent Jennings focused on Ron, knowing it was him by his photo, even though the picture was an old one. He hadn't changed much over the years.

"I'm Ron Powers. What can I do for you?"

"It's been brought to our attention that you were a former member of the Black Panther Party."

"That was a long time ago. I was a kid. What about it?"

"Old enough to get arrested."

"Your point."

"It's also been brought to our attention that you have a supplier that has connections to the Middle East."

Ali dropped his arms and took a step forward. "What the hell are you talking about?"

Ron backed him up with his arm.

"No need to get nasty," agent number two chimed in.

Ali cut the agent a look.

"I don't know what you're talking about and, if my supplier does have these alleged connections, I don't have anything to do with that."

"That's where you're wrong," Agent Jennings said.

"We want to take a look at your books and your employee list," Agent Collins said.

"You got a warrant?"

Jennings tightened his face. "It won't be a problem to get one if you force us to go that route."

"No force. Just citizens' rights. What's left of them," Ron tossed back.

"It's really best if you don't make this more difficult than it is," said Collins. "You'll make us start thinking you have something to hide."

"Go get your warrant," Ali challenged.

"What's your name?" Collins asked.

"Malcolm X."

"Very funny. We'll be back—with a warrant," Collins said.

"You do that." Ron watched them leave before kicking his chair clear across the room. It slammed against the wall and flipped over. He threw his hands up in the air and began turning in a slow circle. "What the hell was that?" He stuck his arm out toward the door then ran his hands across his head. "I don't believe this crap. The Panthers, I was seventeen damned years old." He looked toward the ceiling. "I know they've never stopped watching and listening. I've seen the 'unmarked' cars from time to time, the clicks on my phone line. But they've never approached me—accused me of something."

"Look, man, you have nothing to hide."

"I know I don't," he snapped. He blew out a breath.

"If they are really investigating and not just trying to give you a hard time, my name is eventually going to come up."

Ron looked at him. "And?"

"Hey, man, you know my slate ain't clean, especially from back in the day."

Ron waved off his concern. "We'll deal with it." He lowered himself into an upright chair. "We need to go through our records. Check our Philly supplier."

"Yeah, and, in the meantime, I suggest you get a lawyer. Just in case."

"You're right. Everybody is so paranoid, these days, there's no telling what those fools might cook up." He slammed his fist down on the desk. "Dammit!"

"Do you have an attorney?"

"Do I look like the kind of guy that keeps an attorney at the end of a phone…just in case?"

"All right, all right, look, we need to find someone."

"Yeah. Hey, Ellie's friend, Ann Marie, her guy is an attorney."

"Can you call him?"

"I'm sure Ellie can get a number for me."

He got up and went to the phone. He dialed the spa, expecting Elizabeth to pick up, but he got Barbara, instead.

"*Pause for Men,* how can I help you? Barbara speaking."

"Hi, Barbara, it's Ron. Can I speak to Ellie?"

Barbara winced. "She's not here right now. Can I give her a message?"

Ron checked his watch. It was barely eleven. "Did she say where she was going or how long she was going to be?"

Barbara started to respond but divine intervention let her off the hook.

"Uh, never mind, I'll call her on her cell. Thanks, Barbara." He hung up and dialed Elizabeth's cell phone. It rang and rang until it went into voice mail. Ron frowned. "Hey, Ell, it's me. Listen, can you give me a call as soon as possible. It's important. Thanks."

Ali returned from the back storage room. "Did you get her?"

"Naw," he said absently, his mind turning in a direction he didn't want to go in. "Left a message for her on her cell."

Ali angled his head to the side. "You cool?"

Ron looked up. "Yeah, yeah. Look, we need to head on over to the construction site."

"Right. Ready when you are."

Ron got his bag, turned off the lights and set the alarm.

Where was Elizabeth?

Elizabeth pulled her car to a stop in front of Matt's apartment, after stopping at the pharmacy to drop off his prescription for antibiotics and pain killers. She'd never been to his new place, and sitting in front of where he now called home was a rude awakening.

During the months of their separation, she'd initially remained in the home, which they'd lived in for more than a decade. After the sale of the house, she'd moved into the apartment above the spa, leaving her life with Matt behind her. Now she was reminded of how far they'd come.

"Thanks," he said, once she'd put the car in Park.

"Can you make it from here?"

"I think so." He dared to look at her. "You want to come in for a minute?"

"I really don't think that's a good idea, Matt."

"Look, we're both adults. I'm not some horny teen that's going to try to get in your pants as soon as you shut the door. Besides, I couldn't, anyway. The least I can do is offer you something to drink."

She pursed her lips in thought. She could tell that as hard as he was trying, he was uncomfortable. What harm could it do? He was still a little shaky in her estimation and she'd never forgive herself if she simply drove off and something happened to him. And someone was going to have to go back to the pharmacy when his prescriptions were ready and Matt certainly wasn't up to it.

"All right. But just for a few minutes—until you get settled. I'll pick up your medicine and then I really have to go."

"Deal." He opened the door and gingerly got out of the car.

She got out after him, set the alarm on her car and followed him into the turn-of-the-century apartment building.

The lobby was something right out of a movie set, with chandeliers hanging from cathedral ceilings, swirling marble floors and gleaming elevators. There was even a horseshoe-shaped desk, shined to such a high gloss that you could see your reflection, and a clerk behind it, complete with a brilliant red jacket with gold buttons and braiding.

"Good afternoon, Mr. Lewis," the clerk greeted.

"Afternoon, Milton."

"I have a package for you, sir." He leaned down behind the desk and handed Matt a large box from Fed Ex.

Elizabeth hurried over and took the box from Matt, giving the clerk a short smile. "Thanks," she murmured.

"Milton, this is my—" he shot Elizabeth a glance "—wife, Elizabeth."

Elizabeth opened her mouth to protest, but held her tongue.

"Pleasure to meet you, finally, Mrs. Lewis."

"Thank you."

Matthew moved toward the elevator. Elizabeth was hot on his heels. But she wouldn't make a scene. At least, not here.

The doors swooshed open.

"I'm on nine," Matthew said, depressing the button.

Elizabeth fumed.

The bell dinged, the doors opened and they stepped out into a lush corridor with carpeting so thick it make the walkway soundproof.

"I'm at the end of the hall, facing the river, actually. Pretty good view," he rambled, fishing for his keys in his pockets.

He opened the door and stepped aside to let Elizabeth pass. She was immediately impressed.

The small foyer with cushioned benches on either side of the archway opened onto the main room, which was straight out of a magazine. Classy, sleek, yet personal. She wasn't sure what she'd expected but it wasn't this. A part of her had hoped that it would be a hovel, dirty clothes and dishes everywhere, the scent of old socks in the air. But it was nothing like that.

The windows arched halfway around the room and the treatment was simple Roman shades in off-white. The furniture was minimal but, she could tell by looking, that it was expensive. The design was a combination of old and new, which gave the room a unique feel. Antique tables embraced a low oxblood leather sectional that could easily seat ten, two swag lamps teased the tiffany shades of tabletop lighting. On the far wall of the room was an entertainment center that looked like the deck of a spaceship with all the lights and gadgets. Then, on the right side, was an intimate dining area. He even had fresh flowers as a centerpiece.

"I'll show you around," he said, after giving her a moment to take in the room. "The kitchen is through that door." The door was virtually invisible when it was closed, blending in perfectly with the décor and the paint.

He pushed open the door to the kitchen. It was small, but state of the art. Everything was stainless steel, from the high-tech oven with the glass range top, to the refrigerator, dishwasher and garbage disposal. The island counter space could be used for food preparation as well as eating.

"The guest bathroom is this way." He pushed through another invisible door that led to a small anteroom that had built-in cabinets on either side. The bathroom was just as fabulous as the rest of·the house, complete with Jacuzzi. "My office is down the hall." He opened the door and showed her his workroom. Sleek and stylish and surprisingly neat. "The master bedroom and bath is on the other side of the hallway."

He turned to her. "That's the grand tour."

"Very nice. If I didn't know better, I'd swear you had a woman living with you."

He chuckled lightly. "Then, I'm sure you wouldn't believe I did this all myself," he said, leading her back to the front of the apartment.

"Did you?"

"Yep. I picked each and every item myself, including the contact paper in the cabinets." He grinned.

"Then, I am impressed. I didn't know you had it in you."

"That's because those were the things you wanted to do. Whenever I offered a suggestion…" He let the sentence drift off.

Elizabeth licked her lips. "I didn't think you were really interested, just humoring me."

He focused in on her. "I wasn't," he said softly.

For a moment, they faced each other in the confines of the anteroom. The space grew smaller, the air hot. Elizabeth's heart began to race. Too many images clouded her mind.

"I better go see if your medicine is ready," she said in a rush, and brushed by him. She practically ran to the front of the apartment, making at least one wrong turn in the process.

She grabbed her bag from the chair where she'd left it and hurried to the front door. She heard him behind her and she opened the door and shut it quickly behind her.

She was breathless by the time she reached the elevator, not from exertion, but from the racing of her heart.

What had almost happened back there? She stabbed the button of the elevator demanding that it arrive.

Finally, the doors opened. She stepped on,

walked all the way to the back and leaned against the wall. She shut her eyes and drew in a long breath. She knew it was a mistake coming here.

She drew in long gulps of air once she got outside in the hopes of clearing her head. Instead of taking the car for the five-block drive, she chose to walk to give herself time to think.

It was over between her and Matt. They were divorced. It was official. She'd tossed her feelings away for him and reinvested them in Ron. So why did she suddenly feel so uncertain? Why did all those old emotions rear their ugly heads when they were in that small space together?

No, she wasn't going to buy into that. It was a vulnerable time for both of them. That was it and nothing more.

She went into the pharmacy, picked up his prescriptions and headed back. As soon as she returned and was assured that he was comfortable she was getting out of there and going back to work.

"Make sure you take them as prescribed," she said, handing him the bag.

"I will." His eyes ran over her, but she refused to meet his gaze.

"Ellie…I want to thank you again."

"Don't worry about it," she said. She wanted to leave.

"Are you involved with someone?"

She was so stunned by his question, it took her a moment to respond.

"Yes."

He nodded and lowered his head. "I see. Well, I hope you're happy—that he makes you happy."

"I'd better go. I really need to get back to work." She headed for the door.

"I'll, uh, let you know what I decide to do, if that's okay."

Her chest constricted as she was brought crashing back to reality. "Yes, of course. I want to know."

"Okay." He opened the door for her. "Drive safely."

She looked at him for a moment, maybe a moment too long then quickly hurried away.

Once within the safety of her car, she released the breath she'd been holding. She gripped the wheel, and realized her hands were shaking. This was the first time she and Matt had been face-to-face in months. It was disconcerting to say the least, notwithstanding the circumstances.

Elizabeth reached inside her purse for her phone. She wanted to call Barbara and let her know she was on her way. When she took out her phone, she saw that she had a message waiting. It must have come through while she was at the hospital and had turned off her phone.

She scrolled through to Messages and recognized Ron's number. Her heart thumped uncomfortably against her chest. According to the time, he'd called more than four hours earlier. There was also a message from Barbara that had come in moments after Ron's. Elizabeth called Barbara back, first.

"Hey, where are you? How is Matt?"

"He's home. Doing okay. All things considered."

"And you?"

"I don't really know. We'll talk when I get there. I'm on my way."

"Ron called here looking for you shortly after you left."

"I see a message on my phone from him. What did he say? Did he tell you why he called?"

"Just that he wanted you to call him. He sounded a little stressed."

"Yeah. Okay. Thanks."

"Are you going to call him?"

"I'll call him when I get back to work. Did he ask where I was?"

"Kind of, but before he waited for me to say

anything, he said he would call you on your cell. I was relieved. To tell you the truth, I didn't know what to tell him."

"I'll be there in about fifteen minutes." She disconnected the call and pulled off from the curb. She should have called Ron and told him where she was going and why. Why hadn't she? It was the same questions she knew Ron was going to ask. What was she going to tell him? And why hadn't she reminded Matt that they were no longer husband and wife?

Chapter 6

Ron tried repeatedly to reach his supplier in Philly but kept getting a recording that the number was out of service. There had to be a mistake, but he didn't have any more time to spend on it. What concerned him more was that he had yet to hear from Elizabeth.

"Hey, Ron," one of his workers called out. "Need you to take a look at this flooring."

"Be right there."

They were working on a five-story brownstone that had been left in disrepair for so long it had been deemed unsafe by Housing Preservation and Development. But the community churches had come together to save it. He wasn't getting paid what he normally would for a job this size, but it was worth it. Had the churches not stepped in he was sure the money men would have then torn it down and put up some co-op, so expensive that no one in the community could afford to live there.

He carefully trotted up the stairs that had just been refinished. Water damage had destroyed so much of the original wood that rehab was taking much longer than usual. The specialty of his business was restoration. His workers took painstaking efforts to find the right replacement materials for every facet of the job to bring the brownstones back to their former glory.

"What's up, Mac?"

"I wanted you to take a look at the supply of wood we received for the floors. It's not what we asked for. Pretty good replica, but it ain't the real thing."

Ron bent down and ran his hand over the wood then compared the supply to some of the old wood that was pulled up. Mac was right. He ran his hand across his face. "What about the rest of the shipment?"

"Everything else looks fine. It's just this batch."

Ron stood. "Okay, for the time being, just leave this part of the job. I'll check into what happened."

"No problem. It's the last thing that needs to be done on this floor, anyway."

Ron looked around. The stained glass was in the windows, the shutters hung, the floor-to-ceiling mantle place had been stripped and re-done and the moldings were completed. "Good job," he said.

"The electrical guys will rehang the chandelier tomorrow."

Ron nodded. "I'll get back to you about the floor." He walked away and ran into Ali on his way down the stairs. "We had a problem," he said. "Actually, we still have one."

"What's up?"

Ron explained about the floor and his inability to get in contact with the supplier.

"What are you thinking?"

"I'm trying not to. Just hoping that it's a major coincidence that the G-men came to see us to talk about the supplier and now, suddenly, I can't get him on the phone. Not to mention that he didn't ship what we paid for."

"Any luck getting in touch with Ellie?"

"No. Not yet."

"Must be a busy day," Ali said.

"Yeah," Ron replied absently, "it must be."

Elizabeth arrived at the spa close to six. Barbara was putting on her jacket.

"Hey, girl. I need to get out of here. Wil is expecting me. Carmen is covering until closing."

"Okay. Thanks for today."

"Sure. You okay?"

"I think so." She hesitated. "No, not really. But I'll work it out."

Barbara checked the overhead clock. She'd promised to meet Wil and his son, Chauncey, for dinner. She wanted to run home and change, first.

"Listen, if you want to talk…"

Elizabeth waved her off. "No, no. You go ahead. You have plans and I've infringed on your day enough as it is."

"Hey, if a friend can't infringe, then who can?" She smiled warmly at Elizabeth.

"I'll be okay. Leave and go see your man, girl."

Barbara grinned. "If you're sure. I can always call him and tell him I'm running late."

"We'll talk tomorrow. That will give me some time to get my head straight."

Barbara blew out a sigh. "Okay." She kissed Ellie's cheek. "Whatever it is, it will be fine."

"I know," she said, but she wasn't too sure about that.

"See you tomorrow."

"Have a good time and tell Wil hello for me."

Elizabeth put her things beneath the desk and took a quick inventory of the space. Busy as usual, but it would wind down soon enough. She plopped down in the chair, suddenly exhausted. She knew she needed to call Ron. Putting it off wasn't going to help, and she certainly didn't want to wait to have him call her again.

She reached for the phone just as two men she'd never seen before came through the doors. She put the phone down. They approached looking a little too stiff around the collar for her tastes.

"Hello, may I help you?"

"Nice place," said the first man, the taller of the two.

"Thank you."

"How long have you been in business?"

"Just under a year. Would you be interested in membership or would you like a tour?"

The second man leaned on the counter and faced her. "Actually, we'd like some information."

"Sure." She reached for a brochure.

"No. Not that kind of information." The first man took out a photo from the breast pocket of his suit and showed it to her.

Her breath caught for a moment. It was a picture of Ron.

"Do you know this man?"

"Why?"

The man who'd produced the photo went back into his pocket and produced his identification. Agent Brian Jennings, FBI.

Elizabeth felt light-headed. She swallowed. "I don't understand."

"It's quite simple, actually. Do you know this man?"

"Uh, yes. Why?"

"We're looking into his activities, and this place is one of them."

"I don't understand."

"According to our information, he was the contractor on the renovation project for this establishment. Is that correct?"

Her pulse was pounding so loud in her ears that she barely heard him.

"Yes."

"Do you have records of his work for you?"

"What kinds of records?"

"Bills of lading, invoices, things like that," the Agent said.

"I suppose so. But I'm not the owner," she said quickly, stalling for time. "The owner just left. I'm sure she'd know where everything is," Elizabeth said, and forced a smile.

Agent Jennings gave her a long look that made her very uncomfortable. "I see," he finally said. "Maybe we should come back when the owner is here. Do you know when that will be?"

"Tomorrow afternoon."

"And the owner's name is?"

"Uh, Barbara Allen."

"Thank you for all your help, Ms…"

"Lewis."

He smiled and the duo walked out.

Elizabeth lowered herself to the seat. Her knees were shaking. The FBI. What could they possibly want with Ron? Or the spa? Now, she really did have reason to call him.

Jennings and Collins stood outside the building.

"She's lying," Collins said. "According to the article in the paper about the place, Ms. Lewis is one of *Pause for Men*'s four owners."

"Yeah." Jennings frowned. "Wonder what else she's lying about." Maybe this investigation wasn't going to be a waste of time, after all.

Chapter 7

On the quick trip home and then the short ride to Wil's apartment, Barbara couldn't shake the uneasy feeling that something was wrong.

She and Elizabeth had been friends for years. They'd grown closer than most sisters and out of their close-knit group, they were the two that connected best with each other. Ellie was her best friend and she knew that the other woman was going through something and that the "something" was more significant than she was letting on. Maybe she should have stayed and talked to Ellie.

Barbara pulled onto Wil's street and slowed down to look for a parking space. If it wasn't too late when she got home, maybe she would give Ellie a call, to let her know that she was there for her and ready to help.

Barbara parked her brand-new cinnamon-toned Lexus sedan. It was a big present to herself for her fiftieth birthday. Every time she slid onto the plush leather seating and eased her chair back, she was in drivers' heaven. She'd finally turned in her ten-year-old Volvo. As much as she'd loved that car, she wanted something new to go with her new life, her new look and her new man.

There were still days that she thought she was dreaming when she realized just how happy she was with Wil and how fate had stepped in and brought them back together after so many years. It wasn't often that you got a second chance in life, and she intended to make the most of it.

Barbara parked the car and walked across the street to Wil's building. She started to ring the bell, but remembered that he'd given her a key a week earlier. She felt a little funny about it, but Wil insisted that his house was hers and she could drop by anytime. She supposed, at some point, she would reciprocate.

She stuck the key in the front door, then took the elevator up to the third floor. She approached his door just as it was pulled open.

"Hey, Ms. Barbara."

Wil's son, Chauncey, leaned down and planted a kiss on her cheek.

"Heading out?" she asked, pleased as always to see Wil's handsome son.

"Yeah, I have a game tonight. Well, not a real game. Practice." He grinned, flashing deep dimples.

"I thought you were going to join us tonight."

"Yeah, maybe another time. Coach told us this afternoon that we have to be there. Big game on Saturday."

"Have a good practice."

"I will," he said, loping off. "Dad's in the living room," he called out.

Barbara shook her head in amazement as she watched him. She'd swear on a stack of Bibles that the boy had grown another two inches since the last time she saw him.

She stepped inside and shut the door. "Wil!" She put her purse and light jacket down on the hall table and walked in.

Wil stuck his head around the corner. A big grin of welcome was plastered on his face.

Barbara's heart skipped a beat. God, how she loved that man.

"Hey, sugah," he said, and rose to greet her. He came right up to her. "Beautiful, just like I pictured you." He lowered his head and took her mouth in a slow, sizzling kiss. His right arm snaked around her waist and pulled her close.

Barbara melted in her arms as easily now as she did the very first time. She pressed closer, needing his warmth, the feeling of total security when she was in his arms and felt his growing erection pressing against her stomach. For a man well into his fifties, Wil Hutchinson had the stamina and virility of a man half his age. He never ceased to amaze and thrill her.

"Hmm," he murmured, slowing easing back. "Good to see you."

She grinned like a schoolgirl and ducked her head. "You, too."

He draped his arm around her shoulder. "Looks like we have the place to ourselves for the evening," he said, leading her into the living room. "Chauncey won't be back for a couple of hours."

She looked up at him. "Are you thinking what I'm thinking?" she asked in a teasing tone.

"Absolutely."

He took her hand, bypassed the living room and took her to his room and shut the door.

Each and every time Wil made love to her, it was like the first time. Her heart raced, her skin grew hot and her knees got weak. When he touched her, she'd get light-headed, as if she'd had too much to drink and she felt as if she was melting from the inside out.

Wil's eyes slow danced over her. He reached out and cupped her cheek in his large palm, and she nestled against it.

"Did I tell you today how much I love you?" he murmured, his voice thick, vibrating right to her center.

"Why don't you tell me now?"

"I love you, Barbara Allen. More than I could ever imagine." He kissed her lightly, once, twice, before letting his tongue stroke her lips then slip inside her eager mouth.

Barbara moaned softly and moved closer. Wil's strong hands roamed along the curve of her spine. She reached for his belt buckle and unfastened it, undid the button and slid the zipper down.

"Why don't I help you out of *your* things?" he said with a wicked grin on his face.

"I was wondering what you were waiting for," she teased.

Wil reached for the hem of her top and pulled it up and over her head then tossed it on a chair. His gaze grew warm as he looked at her. She felt it all the way down in her soul. He unsnapped her bra with the expertise that came with age and experience. It fell to the floor at their feet. His thumbs brushed across her nipples and her entire body trembled.

Barbara pushed his pants down, letting them bundle at his feet. He stepped out of them. She grabbed his T-shirt and pulled it over his head.

Wil stared into her eyes while he eased down and raised her skirt up above her hips. He hooked his fingers around the elastic of her panties and pulled them off, never taking his eyes off her face. Her breathing escalated. The blood pounded in her head.

Wil lowered himself until he was on his knees in front of her. He pressed his face to her center and inhaled the sweetness of her essence. Her thighs began to tremble. He held her firmly in his hands as he tenderly tasted her.

"Ooh," she moaned, gripping his shoulders to keep from falling.

He teased and played, darted and danced until he knew she was weak, wet and ready.

Barbara's head was spinning. She didn't even

realize that Wil had carried her to the bed. Her skirt was still hiked up around her waist and it was a major turn on. She almost felt like a horny teen in the backseat of her daddy's Coupe deVille.

"My woman," Wil said, his voice thick with desire. He braced his weight above her.

She raised up to kiss his mouth while spreading her thighs to invite him in. When she felt him push against her, she wanted to scream in anticipation. But nothing could compare to the bliss of feeling him slowly fill her, inch by inch until there wasn't even air between them.

For several moments, neither of them moved, both relishing the joy of their union. Then, as if a silent cue had been struck, they moved against each other slow and deliberate savoring the push and pull.

Barbara arched her hips higher, the better to feel all of him. Wil buried his head in the hollow of her neck, placing tiny teasing kisses there.

"I love you," she whispered in his ear.

"I know," he whispered back, and took her higher.

Like a salsa dance, the beat picked up, the pace increased with their desire. The room grew hotter. The sounds of their blended moans intensified.

Barbara's body tingled all over. It started at the balls of her feet and shimmied up her legs. Her thighs spread wider, her knees drew higher.

Wil felt her grip him from the inside and he nearly lost his mind. Barbara's cries of joy filled his ears, entered his soul and rushed out in a powerful gush to fill her with all the love he felt in his heart.

He reared against her, over and over. She yelled out his name as the power of her climax left her trembling and as weak as newborn baby.

Wil collapsed against her, and she held him, stroking his head and sighing contentedly.

"It can't get better than this," he said, his voice thick.

Barbara giggled. "We say that every time."

Wil leaned up so he could look at her. "Yeah, we do, don't we?"

They laughed and held each other.

Barbara emerged from the bathroom after freshening up. She returned to the bedroom to find Wil still stretched out with his hands tucked behind his head, looking very pleased with himself.

"Not bad for an old man," he said, grinning.

Barbara chuckled and came to sit next to him. "There's nothing old about you." She reached for her panties and slipped them back on then found her bra and shirt and continued getting dressed. "You better put something on. I'd hate for Chauncey to come home and find you naked. No telling what he might think."

"He'll think that his old man's still got it going on."

Barbara tossed a pillow at him. "You're terrible." She adjusted her clothing. "And besides, I'm starved."

"Yeah, me, too," he said, finally sitting up. "Want to go out and grab something to eat?"

"Sure. It's a beautiful night. I love spring evenings," she said.

"Sounds like a plan. We can find something up on Amsterdam or Morningside."

They walked up the hill, hand in hand to a new Caribbean restaurant.

"I've heard good things about this place," Barbara said once they were seated.

"At this point, and as hungry as I am, so long as it is hot, I'm good."

They placed their orders and waited.

"We got some bad news today," Barbara said as she sipped her glass of water with a twist of lemon.

Wil frowned with concern. "What?"

"Matt, Ellie's ex-husband…"

"Yeah?"

"He has prostate cancer."

Wil's expression pinched. "Wow, sorry to hear that. How's Ellie taking it? I mean, I know they are not together or anything, but…"

"I think she's pretty shook up. He had the biopsy done today and he called wanting her to be there."

"Did she go?"

Barbara nodded, yes.

"Hmm. Unfortunately, it's a disease that kills a lot of black men."

"I know," she said, her voice filled with sadness. "Have you been tested?"

"Yep. Once a year. So far, so good." He crossed his fingers. "Hopefully, they caught it in enough time to treat it."

"So do I." She waited a beat. "But there was something else…"

Their food arrived. She waited until the waitress left them.

"I don't know, maybe I shouldn't say anything but…"

"You can tell me anything, you know that. So what is it? Are you sick?"

"No, nothing like that." She'd had her own

scare a few months back when she'd found a lump. Fortunately, it was benign but she'd been extra vigilant ever since. "Well, it's about Ellie. You know, she and Ron are really involved. He's asked her to marry him and everything."

"Right."

"Well, when she went to the hospital to be with Matt, she didn't tell Ron that she was going. He'd called the spa looking for her. Thank goodness I didn't have to tell him where she was. But, well…I guess what's troubling me is I'm wondering why she didn't tell him."

His brows rose and fell. "It is kinda touchy. Exes are always a threat in the 'new' person's mind. There's always the thought that they might get back together. Especially, two people who were married and have kids together. There's always that connection. It can be a bit intimidating, at times. Maybe she didn't know how Ron was going to react."

Barbara shrugged slightly. "I guess. I suppose, I'm just feeling that, if you're going to be in a relationship with someone and you want it to work, you have to be honest with each other and just deal with the issues on the table. I couldn't force her to tell him, but I'd hoped she would do the right thing."

"It may be the right thing to you. Unfortunately, everyone doesn't look at things the same way."

"That's true." She sighed, then speared a piece of stewed chicken with her fork and slowly lifted it to her mouth. "We don't have that problem, do we?"

"What problem?"

"Keeping things from each other."

For a moment, he looked like he'd been caught stealing. He swallowed his mouthful of seasoned rice. He reached for his glass of water and took a long drink before answering. He put the glass down.

"Actually, there is something I wanted to talk to you about," he said.

Her heartbeat kicked up a notch. "What is it?"

"I've been thinking of retiring."

Relief rushed through her. "Oh. Is that all? You scared me for a moment."

He took a breath. "That's not really all of it."

She put down her fork and focused on him. "I'm listening."

"I, uh, never thought that New York was a place to grow old in. I have some property down in Charlotte, North Carolina."

She didn't like where this was going.

"And I've been slowly building on it for the past two years. Actually, I started after I was able to put the money into it." He swallowed. "The house will be finished this summer," he quickly added, then looked at her. Her expression was frozen.

Barbara didn't know what to think or what was coming next. But she was pretty sure she wasn't going to like it.

Wil folded his hands atop the table. "I'm planning to put my retirement papers in at the end of the month at the post office. Get things settled up here, get Chauncey off to college in August… and then I want to move to North Carolina," he said.

All of the air left her body. She couldn't have been more stunned if he'd jumped up and slapped her. "Wh-what? Move to North Carolina?" She shook her head in confusion. "What are you talking about?" Her stomach was in a knot. Nothing was making sense.

"I should have told you all this in the beginning. But it seemed so far off at the time. This is something I'd been working on long before we got together, babe. I want something for myself. I'm tired of renting, tired of the daily grind. I want to sit in my backyard, not on a slab of concrete. I've worked hard for this. And, bottom line, when I'm gone, I want my son to have something."

"I see," she said tightly. She wouldn't scream, she wouldn't cry. If this is what he wanted, then so be it. She knew what it was like to have a dream. It was that way for her with the spa. She could understand, even though it was killing her inside. "It sounds…great. Really. I'm happy for you."

"I want you to come with me. I want it to be our house, our future."

"Come with you? But…my life, my business, my friends, my job, everything is here," she said.

"Where do I fit in?"

She blinked rapidly. "In that part I said about 'my life.'"

He reached across the table and took her hand, surprised to find that it was icy cold. "We can make a *new* life, together. Me and you."

"Wil… I…" She blew out a breath.

"Look, you don't have to make a decision right this minute. Think about it. Please?" he said as he gazed deeply into her eyes.

She stared down at her overflowing plate of food and lost her appetite. "Sure. I'll think about it," she murmured. But, even as she agreed to that small thing, she knew that, whatever decision she made, it was going to permanently change their relationship—one way or the other.

Chapter 8

Ron had seen Elizabeth's number come up on his cell phone on his drive home from the work site. By the time she'd finally gotten around to calling him it was close to ten o'clock. He didn't know whether to stay pissed off or to be relieved.

He pulled up in front of his building and hopped out of his car. It had been a helluva day on several fronts and, before he spoke to Ellie and said something he might regret, he opted for a quick, hot shower and a stiff drink.

As he walked through his door, tossing his jacket and knapsack on the couch, the landline rang. His jaw clenched. He walked over to the wall phone in the small efficiency kitchen. The number flashing on the caller ID was Ellie's home number.

Grinding his teeth back and forth, he snatched up the phone.

"Yeah," came his terse greeting.

"Ron, it's Ellie."

He was silent.

"I'm sorry I didn't get to call you earlier. I promise, I will explain everything, but something more important came up."

What could be more important than telling him why it took her all day and half the evening to get back to him and why she wasn't at work.

"Two guys from the FBI came to the spa today."

He sputtered a curse. "When?"

"Early this evening, maybe about five-thirty, six o'clock. Ron—Why are they looking for you?"

This was getting ugly. He blew out a breath of frustration. "I'll tell you about it later. What did they say?"

"They asked to see our invoices and bills of lading from your company."

He rocked his head back and squeezed his eyes shut. "What did you tell them?"

"I told them that they'd have to get it from the owner. I didn't know what else to do."

"Shit! Okay, look, I just walked in the door. Let me shower, change and I'll come over there."

"All right. Ron, what is going on?"

"That's what I'm trying to find out. I'll see you in about an hour." He hung up the phone then banged his fist into the wall.

Ellie's next call was to Barbara. She had to tell her what was going on as soon as possible. Hopefully, she'd decided to come home and not spend the night at Wil's.

Barbara's phone rang and rang until her voice mail kicked in.

"Barb, it's Ellie. Listen, if you get in before midnight, please call me at home. Or first thing tomorrow morning, before you go to work. Thanks." She hung up.

She wasn't sure if Ron had eaten dinner. He said he'd just gotten in. Maybe she could soften the blow by at least fixing him something to eat. She went into the kitchen to see what she could whip up quickly that would not be too heavy at this time of night.

Hunting around in the fridge, she took out the plastic container of chicken, which she'd diced,

After Dark

seasoned and grilled the day before. She took out the lettuce and tomatoes and prepared a salad. She put on a pot of water to boil and added two eggs. It wasn't gourmet, but it would be filling.

Once she was done in the kitchen, she went to change her clothes into a loose-fitting pair of sweats and a T-shirt that read I Luv Books.

The evening was still warm, so she went around the apartment opening the windows just a bit, then she straightened the magazines in the rack and reorganized some of her CDs that were out of the cases. Turning around in a slow circle with her hands on her hips, she realized she'd finally run out of things to occupy her mind and her nervous fingers. She was a wreck on several fronts. That was a fact that she couldn't escape.

Feeling suddenly overwhelmed, she plopped down on the couch and pointed the remote at the flat screen television. She clicked right by all the news broadcasts hoping to land on something mind numbing like music videos.

She finally settled on watching a rerun of an awards show when the phone rang in concert with the doorbell. She reached for the phone, taking it with her as she walked to the intercom.

"Hello?" she said into the phone. "Who?" Into the intercom.

"It's Matt, Ellie."

Dammit.

"It's me, Ron."

She pressed the door buzzer. She had about two minutes before Ron got upstairs.

"Matt, what is it? Are you okay?"

"I'm not feeling very well," he managed to get out.

"Matt, do you need to call your doctor?"

"I already did. He told me to meet him at the hospital. I feel so…sick. I know I can't make it there on my own. Can you—"

She cut him off before he could get the request out. "I can't, Matt. Call a car service. Or, if you feel that badly, call 9-1-1 and let them send an ambulance."

She heard what sounded like retching on the other end. There was a knock on her front door. All she needed now was a swarm of locusts.

"Call the car service, Matt. I'll check on you in the morning." She hung up and went to the door, her conscience kicking her all the way. She pulled the door open.

"Hi," she mumbled, and turned away.

"Hmm, good to see you, too," he said in re-

sponse to the chilly greeting. He shut the door.
Well, if it's like that, he thought, they both had
bones to pick.

"I fixed you something to eat. It's in the
kitchen if you're hungry."

"What about you?"

"I'm okay," she said, with a toss of her hand
into the air. She went into the living room. Ron
followed her.

"We need to talk, Ellie."

She whirled toward him. "Yeah, I'd say we do."

Ron came to the love seat and sat down. He
rested his forearms on his thighs. "Guess I'll go
first."

Elizabeth pursed her lips and sat down opposite him, thankful for her momentary reprieve.

He told her about his visit earlier in the day
from the two agents, who'd inadvertently accused him of accepting payments and shipments
from someone they had under suspicion for illegal activities—his supplier.

"What did they do, pick your name out of a
hat?"

"Remember when I told you that, ever since
my days with the Panthers, I get these periodic
checkups—it could be a call or an appearance by
someone unfamiliar. But I know I've been

watched through the years." She listened as he continued. "Well, with all the stepped-up surveillance programs with Homeland Security, apparently, my name put up a red flag when it was connected to my supplier."

"Who is your supplier?"

"This guy in Philly."

"How well do you know him?"

"I don't. He's just a guy I've been using."

"This is crazy. Now they want to investigate the spa and our connection to you. I have yet to let Barbara and the girls know."

"I need an attorney," he cut in. "I was hoping you could put me in touch with Ann Marie's guy, Sterling."

"Sure. I'll let her know to have him contact you."

"The sooner, the better," he said warily. "That was one of the reasons why I'd called you earlier," he said, turning the spotlight on her.

She squirmed a bit in her seat. "I was going to tell you about that."

"I'm listening."

She pushed out a breath. "This morning I got a call from Matthew…"

Ron's brows rose as she spoke. A part of him was saddened for her ex. You wouldn't wish cancer on anyone. But another part was disappointed. This was the second time that she'd hidden something from him regarding her ex-husband, which made him wonder if there was still something between them.

"Why didn't you just tell me, Ell?" he asked once she was done.

"I—I wanted to. I'd started to, but everything happened so fast."

"Ellie, if we're going to do this thing together, we have to trust each other." He looked at her for a long moment. "Do you still have feelings for him."

Her head jerked up. "No. Of course not. Not like that."

He slowly nodded his head.

"He just called," she confessed. "While you were ringing the bell."

"And?"

"He sounded really sick. He wanted me to go with him back to the hospital. I told him to take a cab," she said, sounding as awful as she felt about what she'd done.

"Do you want to go, Ellie?"

She looked into his eyes, trying to gauge his real feelings. "He doesn't have anyone else…" she managed to get out.

Ron stood. "Then, you should go. Have you told the girls what's going on?"

She shook her head. She knew she would have to tell their twin daughters if Matt hadn't. They deserved to know.

"Maybe the two of you need to talk about telling your kids," he said, his tone as tight as a drumskin.

She tugged on her bottom lip with her teeth.

"Why don't you change your clothes and go on over to the hospital?" he said.

She got up and went to him. She pressed her head to his chest, hoping that he would wrap his arms around her and tell her that everything was going to be all right. But he didn't. He just stood there until she moved away. She backed up and looked into his eyes. And, for the first time since they'd been together, she didn't see herself reflected there and it frightened her.

She turned away. "I'm going to change. I'll be right back."

When she returned several minutes later, Ron was gone.

Chapter 9

Elizabeth careened between tears and confusion on her drive to the hospital. She swiped at her eyes and sniffed hard. This was all getting so crazy. She wasn't quite sure how she'd expected Ron to react. Maybe it was best that he left, but what had he been thinking when he did?

He'd asked the question that had been nagging at her constantly: *Was she still in love with Matt?* If she was, did that make her a fool for still loving a man that had hurt her in the worst way? And, if she was, what about her feelings for

Ron? Were they real? Could you love two men at the same time?

Her head began to pound, the onset of a major headache was settling behind her lids. She pulled into the visitors section of the parking lot at the hospital and went straight to the emergency entrance. As she pushed through the doors, she realized that she hadn't even called Matt back to see if he'd come.

Well, she was here now. She headed to the information desk. The woman behind the counter pointed her in the direction of the emergency waiting area. Several rows of patients were waiting in varying stages of illness. She found a nurse and asked about Matthew Lewis.

"I believe he's in exam three. The doctor is with him. But you can't go back there."

"I'm…his wife. Mrs. Lewis."

The nurse looked at her for a moment. "Wait here." She left Elizabeth and pushed through a swinging door.

Moments later, the nurse returned. "Come with me."

Elizabeth followed her into the examination area and was shown to the room where Matthew was. She eased back the drape. Matthew was sitting up on the exam table. Both he and the doctor turned.

"Mrs. Lewis. Come in."

She looked at Matt, who looked the worse for wear, and her heart ached in her chest.

"First, he's going to be all right. He had a bad reaction to the medications. I've lowered the dosage and given him something to combat the nausea."

Elizabeth nodded, all the while looking at Matthew. The sudden, powerful urge to put her arms around him filled her to a point of bursting. Maybe the papers did say that they were no longer legally bound, but she knew, deep inside, that they would always be linked together. No amount of paper or legal jargon would change that. The acceptance of that stunned her, leaving her feeling incredibly uncertain.

"Thanks for coming, Ell."

She swallowed over the tightness in her throat. "How are you feeling?"

"Better."

"Can he go home?"

"I want to monitor him for about another hour and then he can go." He looked from one to the other, his expression severe. "You really must come to a decision about treatment. I cannot impress that upon you enough. Time is the great pretender. You always believe you have plenty of it. I'll be back to check on you," the doctor said, and then he walked out, leaving them alone.

Elizabeth walked farther into the tight space. She didn't know what to say.

"All this has happened so fast," he began. "I mean, I just got the test results back two days ago. Then the biopsy…" He looked up at her. "I can't seem to process it all."

"I know," she said gently, "but this is your life, Matt. You have to decide what you want to do."

"Have you told the girls?"

"No."

"They're going to need to know, even if they don't care."

"Matt," she admonished, "why would you say such a thing? Of course they care. You're their father. They love you."

"Even after everything I've done?"

She averted her gaze for an instant. "They're grown women, Matt. They understand that… things happen in a marriage—to a family."

"I never told them how sorry I was that I hurt you—hurt them."

"I'm sure they know," Elizabeth said.

"What do you think I should do—about the course of treatment?"

She sighed heavily. "I don't know." She placed her hand on his thigh. "Maybe we can talk to the doctor about it…together." She watched his nostrils flare and his eyes fill.

"Thank you," he said, barely able to get the words out.

She nodded. "It's going to be all right. I know it is," she said, as much in statement as in prayer.

He placed his hand atop hers and squeezed it gently.

By the time Elizabeth got back home, it was after midnight. She was exhausted, physically and emotionally. She checked her voice mail. No call from Ron, but Barbara had called. She knew it was much too late to reach her now. She'd call first thing in the morning. Maybe they could get together for breakfast and talk. She had a laundry list of things she needed to get off her chest.

Dragging through the apartment, she stripped out of her clothes and crawled into bed. But once there, with the lights out and only the distant sounds of the streets below to keep her company, she couldn't sleep.

She felt totally overwhelmed, as if she was sinking and had forgotten how to swim. Every time she tried to get her head above water, she got tugged right back down again.

Ron.

Matthew.

She saw herself running through the woods, darting around trees and leaping over foliage until she finally reached a clearing. At the crest of a rolling hill, she spotted two images and recognized them as Matthew and Ron, standing side by side. Seeing them gave her some momentary sense of peace. She started to run toward them and, as she got closer, she realized that they weren't standing on the top of a hill, but on the edge of a cliff. The wind suddenly gusted. Matt and Ron rocked back and forth, losing their balance. She ran faster, but they continued to get farther and farther away. She finally reached the edge of the cliff and stretched out her hands to keep them from falling. Their fingers touched. She almost had both of them. She could save them both if they would just grab hold. And then the wind whipped up again, more powerfully this time, and they were lifted off their feet. Both men began to fall and as they fell she was dragged down with them. She screamed and jumped up from her nightmare.

Her eyes darted around the darkness. Her heart raced out of control. She drew her knees to her chest and lowered her head, drawing in long breaths, hoping to slow her racing heartbeat down.

It was just a dream, she kept repeating to herself. Just a dream.

What was left of the night was spent half sleeping, half waking, the fear of revisiting her dream enough to keep true sleep at bay.

Unable to stay in bed any longer, she stumbled into the bathroom and got into the shower. Feeling mildly refreshed, she fixed a pot of coffee. It was just about seven when her phone rang.

"Hello?"

"Hey, Ell, it's Barbara. I tried you last night."

"Girl, we gotta talk. Wanna have breakfast?"

"My sister in spirit. Come by my house. I'll fix us something while you're on your way."

"Great. See you in about a half hour."

She grabbed her mug of coffee and took it into the bedroom to sip while she got dressed. The forecast called for a chance of showers so she snatched up her umbrella on the way out. The spa wasn't scheduled to open until noon and it would close at ten. Tonight was their late night. At least, the long hours would give her and Barbara a chance to really talk, which reminded her that she needed to get in contact with Ann Marie as soon as possible.

When she knocked on Barbara's door, she could smell the warm scent of fresh biscuits and her stomach yelped in appreciation.

"Hey, girl, come on in."

They swapped cheek kisses.

Elizabeth dropped her umbrella in the bin by the door and followed her nose to the kitchen.

"You can take out the fruit salad from the fridge and help yourself," Barbara said.

"Thanks. How long for those biscuits?"

Barbara chuckled. "About ten minutes. How 'bout an egg-white omelet?"

"You hear me saying no?"

They both laughed.

Elizabeth fixed her bowl of fruit then helped Barbara cut up the ingredients for the omelet. They worked quietly side my side in sisterly companionship, the chatter from the *Steve Harvey Morning Show* entertaining them in the background.

"So, who's first?" Barbara finally said.

"My story is so long I wouldn't know where to begin."

"Guess that leaves me." She filled their plates

with biscuits and eggs and took them to the table and sat down. "Wil plans to move to North Carolina," Barbara said, without further preamble.

"What?"

Barbara nodded. "He dropped that bomb on me last night."

"I don't understand. Just like that? What about his job, his son? What about you?"

"He's putting in his retirement papers at the end of the month. Apparently, he's been having the house built for the past couple of years and it will be finished this summer. Chauncey will be off at college..."

"And you?"

"He wants me to come with him," Barbara said.

Elizabeth's first thought was that she was losing her best friend. She knew it was selfish, but she couldn't help it. "What are you going to do?"

"I have no idea. It's a big decision and it's not like he asked me to marry him or anything. He asked me to move in with him. And I am too old to be shacking up with anybody."

"But...what if he leaves and you don't go? Are you ready to handle that?"

"I've just gotten used to having him back in my life. I've been so happy. I would have to give up everything."

"But you'd have each other," Elizabeth offered.

"It just seems so unfair."

"Life is a bitch…"

"And then you die…"

They chuckled without much humor.

"When do you have to decide?"

"I guess I have a few months, at least. But I know I can't put it off indefinitely, as much as I'd like to. If I do decide to leave there are so many things I'd have to put in order."

Elizabeth was quiet. She couldn't imagine her days without Barbara. They shared such a special bond. Barbara was her rock and she knew that, at any time, day or night Barbara would be there. And not just for her, Barbara was there for all of them.

"Maybe he will ask you to marry him," Elizabeth finally said. "If he did, would you go then?"

Barbara looked at her friend of more than twenty years. "That's the million-dollar question. I guess, I'll play the waiting game for as long as I can."

Elizabeth nodded.

Barbara exhaled. "So, enough about me and my drama. What's going on with you?"

By the time Elizabeth finished detailing the

events of the past day, Barbara's head was spinning. Matthew, Ron, The FBI. *Lawd.*

"I...don't even know what to say, where to start."

"Besides everything else, we've got to deal with this investigation thing. That scares me."

"You!" Barbara bit down on her bottom lip. "Let me call Ann Marie." She got up from the table to make the call.

Ann Marie answered the phone, sounding the way she usually did this time of the morning, like she'd just had the greatest sex in the world. Her soft Caribbean accent purred through the phone.

"I hope Sterling is there with you sounding like that, Ann," Barbara began.

Ann Marie giggled. "Of course, chile', where else 'im gwon be?"

"Listen, sorry to call you so early, girl, but I really need to speak with Sterling. It's a legal matter."

She heard some rustling and muttering then Sterling picked up the phone, his voice still thick with sleep.

"I just want to warn you that my rates are triple at this time of the morning," he teased. "What can I do for you?"

"Yesterday, we had a visit from the FBI..."

She could hear the rustling as Sterling sat up. "I'll make some inquiries when I get into the office. I'll give you a call this morning," he said.

"Thanks, Sterling."

"You have a number for Ron? I need to speak with him."

Barbara handed the phone to Elizabeth who gave him Ron's cell number.

"One crisis put on hold," Barbara said after they finished with Sterling. "Now, back to you and Ron. He just left after you told him you were going to the hospital to see Matt?"

"Yep, I came out of my room and he was gone."

"Have you called him?"

"No."

"Don't you think you should, Ell?"

"I've never been in a situation like this. It's all so alien to me. I mean, Matt was my first love, my husband for twenty-five years. Never, in my wildest dreams, did I ever think I would find myself in a position of trying to decide if I was still in love with my husband or another man. It's supposed to be over between us." She looked at Barbara with pleading eyes.

"Apparently it isn't," Barbara said softly.

Elizabeth lowered her head. "I don't think so,

either. That's what scares me." She told Barbara
about her dream, how real it felt. "I was trying
to save them both. They both needed me…"

"Ell, they are grown men. Men who have to
make their own decisions and live with the out-
comes. You can't be expected to save them,
because you can't. They have to do that for themselves. The person you have to concentrate on is
you. You need to make the right decisions for
you."

"How will I know I'm making the right decision?" Elizabeth asked, her voice aching with
uncertainty.

"You'll know. You'll know."

Barbara sounded so sure, Elizabeth thought as
she picked through her food. But she certainly
wasn't—far from it.

Chapter 10

Barbara wished that she could go directly to the spa with Elizabeth just in case they had another visit, but she was due at the hospital for a morning shift. Actually, she was looking forward to it. One of her favorite patients, Veronica Wells, was scheduled for her therapy. Just thinking about the feisty Veronica made her smile. Veronica was probably close to ninety, but she didn't look a day over fifty. And her exuberant attitude toward life added to the older woman's youthful aura.

As she walked through the corridors of the

Medical Center en route to the rehabilitation wing, she realized how much she truly loved what she did. As a rehabilitation specialist, she'd helped so many people regain or attain a normal way of life. True, she couldn't help everyone, but she could certainly make all their lives more comfortable.

Barbara clocked in at the front desk and went to change into her scrubs. When she returned, her new assistant, Wendy, told her that Mrs. Wells was waiting in the treatment room.

"Thanks." She pushed open the door and Veronica turned to her with a big smile on her face.

"My favorite therapist. The only person I let rub all over me besides my hubby." She giggled like a young girl.

Barbara smiled and closed the door behind her.

"How are you, my dear?"

"Just wonderful. But you aren't. I can tell, you know," Veronica said, wagging a finger at her.

It was amazing to Barbara how well Veronica was always able to read her.

"Now, why would you say that?" Barbara hedged.

"Because I know women in general, that's

why, and I know you, in particular. You show your feelings in your eyes. So rub me down and tell me all about it."

Barbara smiled inside. Veronica Wells was just the medicine she needed today. She prepared Veronica for her exercises and began telling her about the dilemma with Wil.

"I don't really see where you have a problem, my dear," Veronica was saying as Barbara stretched her leg to a ninety-degree angle. "You obviously have a man who loves you and who you love in return. Right?"

"Yes."

"And, take it from me, love doesn't come easy. You're one of the lucky ones. You got a second chance to make it right with the man of your dreams."

Barbara had thought the same thing.

"And the sex is good, right? Because that's important, I don't care what those women's magazines say."

Barbara bit back a smile. "Yes, the sex is wonderful."

"If your friends are true friends they will always be your friends," she continued. "And this job… Ha, as fast as you walk out the door, someone else will walk right in and take your place.

Life is too short. We have to grab happiness when we can."

"But I just started a brand-new business. What about that?"

"And you have three friends who can run it. Next question."

Barbara huffed.

"The bottom line is, you have to make a decision that you are happy with. If you let him go, you'll forever ask yourself 'what if?' You already know you're a great therapist. You already know you have wonderful friends. You already know you can run a business. But what you don't know is if you're still good at a man and woman relationship. And that's what's scaring you."

Barbara lowered Veronica's leg and gently massaged her hip. Was she afraid? Was that really it? She'd been so sure about Michael. She'd taken everyone's advice and jumped into a relationship with a man ten years her junior. She did love him—in a way. But there was always that nagging voice of doubt that kept telling her it wouldn't work—even after she'd accepted his proposal of marriage. Maybe that mistake affected her more than she realized.

And maybe she was letting that recent mistake

with Michael guide her decision about her relationship with Wil.

"As always you are a treasure trove of advice," Barbara said.

"Listen to me, sweetie. I can tell you anything. The next person can tell you something else. But all the answers are inside of you. You'll make the right decision and, even if you don't, you'll bounce back. We all do."

Perhaps, Barbara thought, but she wasn't sure if she had enough spring left in her to bounce back after another fall.

She had two more patients to attend to before she could leave and head over to the spa. Her morning had been so busy, she hadn't had a chance to check in with Elizabeth to see if they had any more visitors. But the person she really wanted to talk with was Sterling. She needed to know her rights when it came to turning over information about Ron. She'd watched enough television crime dramas to know that they couldn't take anything without a warrant. But what if they came with a warrant? And how involved would the spa become in the investigation if the did try to pursue anything?

The questions ran around in her head. After all the work they'd put into getting *Pause for Men* up and operational, there was no way in hell she was going to let it be ruined.

She could sure use Stephanie right about now. If there was ever anyone who could put a good spin on a crappy situation, it was Stephanie. If things got ugly she'd have to use her skills as a public-relations genius to make the spa smell like roses and not old gym shoes.

After several tries, she finally found a parking space and headed inside to the spa. As usual, it was busy. That was a good thing.

Elizabeth wasn't at the front desk. "Hey, Carmen, where's Ellie?"

"Oh, hey, Barbara. She went down to the office."

"Thanks. I'll be right back." She put her things under the desk then went downstairs.

The office door was closed. She knocked lightly.

"Come in."

"Hey," she said, then stopped when she saw Elizabeth on the phone.

"So, I'll see you later?" Elizabeth was saying. "Okay." She hung up the phone. "That was Ron. We're going to talk tonight. And Sterling called. He said he was going to come by later on this afternoon when he leaves court."

"Okay. No surprises, so far, right?"

"None, so far," Elizabeth replied.

"So, what did Ron say?" Barbara asked.

"That he had some thinking to do and he'd talk to me about it this evening."

Barbara patted her arm. "It's all going to work out. I guess, the last person Ron expected to pop back in your life was Matt."

"Hmm. True. Him and me, both."

"You have some thinking to do, yourself," Barbara said.

"I know."

"I got some of the best advice anyone could offer this morning at the hospital."

"From one of the staff?"

"No. Actually, from a patient." Barbara grinned. "She is my absolute favorite. Anyway, she said I already know what I have, I know what I can accomplish, but what I don't know is if I'm still good at a relationship and that's what's scaring me. In my case, it's leaving everything that's familiar. And, for you, it's going back to what *is* familiar even if it's not good for you."

Elizabeth thought about what Barbara said for a moment. "I never looked at it that way."

"But, as always with Veronica, she said go for happiness 'cause life is too short," Barbara said.

"That, I can definitely agree with."

"Hey, hey, hey, isn't anyone going to welcome me with open arms?"

They both turned to see the ever-stylish Stephanie breeze through the door. On first blush, Stephanie Moore could easily be mistaken for supermodel turned talk-show host, Tyra Banks. As always, she looked fabulous.

"Steph!" they sang in harmony.

Stephanie rushed over and got a group hug.

Barbara held her back at arms length. "You look good, girl. When did you get back?"

"Last night. I wanted to surprise everybody."

"So…are you, or aren't you?"

"Is she, what?" Elizabeth asked.

"Well, I guess I can tell you now. Before I left for Texas to see my dad, I thought I was pregnant."

Elizabeth's eyes widened in surprise. "And?"

"Well, ladies, get your acts together 'cause you're going to be aunties in about seven months!"

They squealed in delight and hugged again.

"This is so exciting," Barbara said. "Oh, I hope it's a girl so I can do shopping for all those tiny girly things," she said, and giggled.

"How does Tony feel about it?" Elizabeth asked.

"Ooh, he's thrilled," she said, grinning.

"So, when is the wedding? You are going to get married, aren't you?" Elizabeth asked, unable to imagine having a baby without a husband, even in this day and age.

"We're talking about it. We just need to decide when."

"Then, we need to plan a wedding, too!" Barbara chirped, clapping her hands in delight. "Not to change the subject from your fabulous news, but how was the visit with your dad?"

For years, Stephanie believed that her father had abandoned her and her twin sister, Samantha, and was dead. It wasn't until Ali, Ron's friend, recognized her as the little girl he used to know that she learned that her dad was in a V.A. hospital in Texas and had been for years.

Stephanie blew out a breath. "It was…hard, scary and eye-opening. We had a wonderful visit. Of course, it's impossible to cover all the years we missed in a short visit, but we sure tried." She smiled softly. "I got my dad back, ya'll," she said as her eyes filled with tears. "And he'll be around to see his grandchild."

"Oh, Steph, I'm so happy for you, girl," Barbara said.

"Me, too," Elizabeth chimed in.

Stephanie sniffed. "So, enough about me. What's been going on around here?"

Barbara and Elizabeth looked at each other, then at Stephanie.

"We have so much to tell you," Barbara said.

"I don't like the sound of that," Stephanie said.

"Trust me, sis, you ain't heard nothing yet."

By the time Barbara and Elizabeth finished bringing Stephanie up to speed, her mouth was hanging open.

"Damn, ya'll, I go away for a couple of weeks and all hell breaks loose." She rubbed her forehead. "How is this investigation, or whatever it is, going to affect our business?"

"We have to be prepared for some kind of fallout if they decide to pursue it. Sterling is going to be here later. I'm sure he'll let us know what our options are," Barbara said.

Stephanie nodded as her thoughts starting turning in PR mode. She was definitely going to have to come up with some kind of spin position in the event that this got in the papers. "I'll meet with Terri and we'll put our heads together." She blew out a breath. "Anything else?"

Barbara and Elizabeth flashed each other another pointed look.

"The rest deserves a 'girlz' night," Barbara said.

"For sure. A welcome back and a catching up session."

"Name the time and place and I'm there."

"Tonight. My house. Eight?" Barbara said.

"Sounds good to me. I'll call Ann Marie and Terri."

Barbara and Elizabeth got up.

"I have a client coming in about ten minutes," Barbara said. "I need to get busy."

"Yeah, and I have a bunch of stuff to check on."

"I'm going to catch up on emails and calls. See you ladies later."

Barbara and Elizabeth walked out.

Stephanie sat down and thought about everything she'd been told. Wow, she'd gotten back just in time.

Chapter 11

Jennings was going over the reports he'd put together on Ron Powers, the supplier and the spa. On the surface, it looked intriguing, but, under close examination, it simply did not hold up. The guy was clean. Hadn't been in any kind of trouble since he was seventeen years old and was arrested during a protest.

It really got under his skin how folks were targeted. Granted, there were a lot of crazies out there. And, yes, terrorists were in their midst, but, in his humble opinion, they wasted much too much time chasing down the good guys. Still, he had a job to do, as distasteful as it was. He'd follow through, dig as far as he could go and, hopefully, Mr. Powers would come out of this and land on his feet. He didn't want to be the one to bring another brother down or possibly ruin a black-owned business. But he also knew he needed his job.

Adam sauntered up to his desk. "How's it going with the case? Anything new?"

"No, not really. I've gone back five years and traced Powers's movements. So far, I haven't come up with anything of interest," Jennings concluded.

"I've been checking out that supplier in Philly, Plez Rhamin," Adam said as he flipped through some papers he was holding in his hand. "Born here, parents born here. Took over his father's lumber business three years ago when the dad passed away."

Jennings looked up at Adam with a sarcastic sneer on his face. "Very chilling information, Adam." He shook his head. "We told those people that we had information on the supplier that was suspect. It was all a crock."

"Only a tactic to see if they were going to spill something," Adam said.

"Spill what? That they're hardworking American citizens who are trying to make decent lives for themselves in the land of plenty? Damn, man what are we doing?"

"What's gotten into you? We're doing our job, that's what we're doing," Adam said.

Jennings pushed up from his swivel chair, sending it spinning in a quick circle. "Yeah, but I ain't gotta like it." He brushed past Adam and walked out of the office.

Sterling Chambers trotted down the steps of the courthouse. Handsome, always impeccably dressed and, with the charisma of a movie star, Sterling flourished in the profession he loved— the law. There was nothing more thrilling to him than standing in front of a room full of people and mesmerizing them, convincing them, changing their minds—with the power of his words.

He'd just won a case for his client, who was being sued in the millions for copyright infringement for his music. They could have settled out of court, but the plaintiffs honestly believed they could win with lies and doctored records. Not on his watch.

Just as he reached the sidewalk, his cell phone rang. He pressed the earpiece to listen as he headed to his car.

An Important Message from the Publisher

KIMANI PRESS™

Dear Reader,

Because you've chosen to read one of our fine novels, I'd like to say "thank you"! And, as a special way to say thank you, I'm offering to send you two Kimani Romance™ novels and two surprise gifts – absolutely FREE! These books will keep it real with true-to-life African-American characters that turn up the heat and sizzle with passion.

Please enjoy the free books and gifts with our compliments...

Linda Gill

Publisher, Kimani Press

Peel off Seal and Place Inside...

PUBLISHERS FREE GIFTS SEAL THANK YOU

We'd like to send you two free books to introduce you to our new line – Kimani Romance™! These novels feature strong, sexy women and African-American heroes that are charming, loving and true. Our authors fill each page with exceptional dialogue, exciting plot twists, and enough sizzling romance to keep you riveted until the very end!

KIMANI ROMANCE ... LOVE'S ULTIMATE DESTINATION

Your two books have a combined cover price $11.98 in the U.S. and $13.98 in Canada, but are yours **FREE!** We even send you two wonderful surprise gifts. You can't los

THE EDITOR'S "THANK YOU" FREE GIFTS INCLUDE:

▶ Two NEW Kimani Romance™ Novels
▶ Two exciting surprise gifts

YES! I have placed my Editor's "Thank You" Free Gifts seal in the space provided at right. Please send me 2 FREE books, and my 2 FREE Mystery Gifts. I understand that I am under no obligation to purchase anything further, as explained on the back of this card.

PLACE
FREE GIFTS
SEAL
HERE

168 XDL ELWZ   368 XDL ELXZ

FIRST NAME

LAST NAME

ADDRESS

APT.#

CITY

STATE/PROV.

ZIP/POSTAL CODE

Thank You!

Offer limited to one per household and not valid to current subscribers of Kimani Romance.
Your Privacy – Kimani Press is committed to protecting your privacy. Our Privacy Policy is available online at www.eHarlequin.com or upon request from the Reader Service. From time to time we make our lists of customers available to reputable firms who may have a product or service of interest to you. If you would prefer for us not to share your name and address, please check here. ☐

▶ DETACH AND MAIL CARD TODAY!

® and ™ are trademarks owned and used by the trademark owner and/or its licensee.

© 2006 Kimani Press.

(K-ROM-07)

If offer card is missing write to: The Reader Service, 3010 Walden Ave., P.O. Box 1867, Buffalo, NY 14240-1867

BUSINESS REPLY MAIL
FIRST-CLASS MAIL   PERMIT NO. 717-003   BUFFALO, NY

POSTAGE WILL BE PAID BY ADDRESSEE

THE READER SERVICE
3010 WALDEN AVE
PO BOX 1867
BUFFALO NY 14240-9952

NO POSTAGE
NECESSARY
IF MAILED
IN THE
UNITED STATES

"Hey, baby," he said at the sound of Ann Marie's voice.

"I'm heading over there now. I just got out of court. Okay, I'll see you when you get back. I guess I'll have to fix my own dinner since you'll be with the ladies tonight," he teased. "Yeah, love you, too." He disconnected the call.

Their relationship had been an uphill battle, one that he didn't think he would win, but he had. For a while, he'd really believed that Ann Marie would go back to her estranged husband, Terrance. It had been messy, but the divorce was finalized, much to his relief. That was all behind them now and he was ready to take the next step with her. He smiled as he opened the door to his Mercedes Benz and slid behind the wheel. Ann Marie had found a place in his soul that he didn't know still existed and every day with her was an adventure.

He pulled off into the early afternoon traffic and his mind immediately shifted to the task at hand. He'd done some preliminary research into the statutes authorizing the Homeland Security Act and it didn't look good for Ron or the ladies. If the FBI came up with a warrant, they would be forced to turn over whatever documents were requested. He hoped it wouldn't come to that and, if it did, he prayed that they wouldn't find anything. He was not an advocate of a country that policed its own citizens, but he also understood that the government was under siege from inside and out. If you had the slightest blip of irregularity from a security standpoint, law-enforcement officials could make your life pure hell.

Sterling arrived at the spa and was amazed at how busy it was in the middle of the day. *Pause for Men* was no regular exercise gym. It was an experience. And an experience that was nice and pricey. Which always made him wonder how did all these money-making men have so much free time on their hands.

"Hey, Drew," he said to the security guard. "Been a while. How are you?"

Drew Hawkins had been hired several months ago when Stephanie was being stalked by her ex-boss and his crazy wife. And according to the pillow talk between him and Ann Marie, Drew was now seeing Ann Marie's daughter, Raquel, although it was supposed to be top secret. Raquel had also been responsible for the interior design of the entire spa.

"Not bad. And yourself?"

"Can't complain. Is Barbara or Elizabeth around?"

"Yeah—" he pointed toward the café "—they're having lunch."

"Thanks." He headed toward the café, one of the highlights of the spa. The menu was stocked with scrumptious health food, courtesy of Elizabeth's twin daughters, Dawne and Desiree, who owned their own restaurant *Delectables*. He had to give credit where it was due, the spa was brimming with talented women. "Good afternoon, ladies. Anyone care to buy me lunch?"

Barbara and Ellie glanced up and smiled.

"Sterling. Have a seat. For you, lunch is on the house," Barbara said.

"You have any news?" Elizabeth asked, her anxiety kicking up a notch upon seeing Sterling and knowing why he'd come.

Sterling sat down on the chair next to Barbara and folded his hands atop the white table.

"The bottom line is if they come back with a warrant, you will have to turn over to them whatever records they ask for. If that happens, I need you to call me immediately. But, before that happens, I want to take a look at all the documents you have relating to Ron. I'm going to have my assistant review them. I'm hoping that she can do the review here. The last thing we'd want is for the Feds to show up and the documents not be here. They'll really sink their teeth into you, then."

"What if they find something?" Elizabeth asked.

Ron pressed his lips together. "If they do, and I'm sure they won't, the spa and the owners could be implicated, perhaps as accessories."

Elizabeth groaned.

"But we didn't do anything," Barbara insisted.

"I know that. But it's just how things work." He held up his hand. "We're getting ahead of ourselves and possibly worrying for nothing. Did these guys leave you a card or anything?"

"Yes. I have it at the front desk," Elizabeth said.

"Good. I'll give them a call. Let them know that any further contact on this matter needs to come through me. You don't have to answer any more questions."

"What if this gets out to our clients?" Barbara asked, her concern growing by the minute.

"We'll deal with that if and when the time comes."

Barbara and Elizabeth were silent for a moment.

Elizabeth looked at Barbara. "I am so sorry for all this."

"Ellie, please, this isn't your fault. If anything, this comes back to me. It was Michael who recommended Ron's company for the renovations in the first place," Barbara said.

"Ladies, ladies, this isn't about blaming anyone. I'm sure Ron is completely innocent of any wrongdoing and it will all come out in the wash. I'm sure he had no way of knowing of any possible dirty dealings through his supplier. It will all get cleared up, I assure you." But even as he said it, he knew how tenacious the government could be, especially now, when everyone was pumped up with paranoia. Too often, innocent people were found guilty simply by virtue of association.

"You're right. We're jumping the gun, blaming him, ourselves." Barbara slowly shook her head with sadness. She looked at Elizabeth and then Sterling. "Is this what we've come to as a country, as a people?" she asked sadly.

"Not if I have anything to do with it," Sterling said. "But, first, before I can battle the big 'dawgs,' a brother needs some nourishment."

They shared a laugh and, for a moment, the mood lightened.

"Pick whatever you want," Barbara said, passing him the menu. "Besides, from what I gather from our girl, Ann Marie, you need your strength," she said with a wink.

Sterling feigned shock. "That woman can't keep a secret."

Barbara checked her watch. "I have a client on the way. So you will have to excuse me."

"And I have to relieve Carmen," Elizabeth said, wiping her mouth with a paper napkin.

Sterling looked up with a pained expression. "Is it something I said?"

"Enjoy your meal. When you're finished, you can take a look at our files. They are all downstairs in the office. Stephanie's down there and she can show you where everything is."

"Great," Sterling said.

"I feel like I'm in the Twilight Zone," Elizabeth said as they walked away. "It's all so unreal."

"I know. But we'll just have to deal with it and move on. I'm going to prepare for my client. I'll see you later." Barbara headed off to the massage and steam rooms in the basement.

Elizabeth returned to the front desk to relieve Carmen.

"There was a message for you while you were at lunch," Carmen said, handing her a slip of paper.

Matthew had called and wanted to speak with her. She briefly shut her eyes. Frying pan, fire, frying pan, fire. Her life had suddenly turned into a series of hot spots and it seemed like no matter where she landed she was going to get burned.

"Thanks, Carmen." She shoved the note into her pants pocket. She'd call Matt later. "Anything I need to know before you leave?"

"There are two new applications on the desk for review. And there are quite a few memberships that are coming up for renewal. I started checking the system to see which ones would be automatically deducted from their credit cards and those we have to contact. I made a list. It's right next to the applications," Carmen told Elizabeth.

"Great. I'll finish those up and start getting the letters out. Thanks," Elizabeth said as she took Carmen's place behind the desk.

"Sure thing. See you tomorrow. Oh, Kayla called, she said she was running a little late, but she promised to be here by four to cover the desk," Carmen said.

"Okay. Now get going before you're late for class."

Carmen waved and hurried out.

Once Carmen was good and seasoned she would make an ideal manager. She had a little more than a year to go in school to get her under-graduate degree in business administration, but there was nothing compared to practical hands-on experience. She was actually getting credit for working at the spa. Kayla on the other hand was more than a work in progress. She had a good heart, but her mind was always elsewhere, spe-cifically, her modeling career. The girl was drop-dead gorgeous, so much so, that she was almost a hazard at the spa. More than one client had got-ten distracted by Kayla while lifting weights.

Elizabeth settled down behind the desk to go over the applications. To date, they had more than two hundred local members and there were at least seventy-five more who came in from out of town on the weekends or dropped in when they came to New York City on business. She had just started the process of entering the new applicants' information into the computer, when Dawne, one of her twin daughters, came breezing into the spa. She was pushing a cart full of supplies for the café.

"Hey, Mom," she beamed.

"Hi, sweetheart." Elizabeth came from around the counter to help.

"I got this," Dawne said as she kissed her mother's cheek.

"I didn't expect to see you today."

"I know. But we're catering a big corporate lunch tomorrow and we knew we wouldn't have time to get over here."

"You two are simply blooming and growing every day," Elizabeth said as she smiled with pride at her daughter.

"We got it honestly from you and Dad; hard work, a good product and honesty pays off. Let me get this inside and reconfirm the inventory. I'm sorry I'm in such a rush, but I have to get back. It's pretty crazy over there."

"I can imagine," Elizabeth said.

Dawne pushed the cart into the café and started unloading.

At some point, she and Matt would have to tell the twins about their father. The last thing she wanted was for them to hear the bad news from someone other than their parents.

Dawne returned to the desk. "Okay, Mom, I'm out of here."

"All right, sweetheart. Will I see you and your sister this weekend?"

"Sure thing. We'll cook."

"Good luck tomorrow."

"Thanks." Dawne kissed Elizabeth's cheek and darted for the door, running smack into Brian Jennings.

Elizabeth's knees got weak, but nothing could prepare her for the hug Dawne gave Brian before taking his hand and leading him over to a stunned Elizabeth. She couldn't breathe.

"Brian, this is my mom, Elizabeth Lewis, she's one of the co-owners."

Elizabeth's heart was racing out of control.

"Mom?" Dawne looked at her mother quizzically.

Elizabeth felt faint. She finally saw Brian's hand extended toward her. She thought she shook it, but wasn't sure until she felt his strong fingers wrap around hers.

"Pleasure to meet you, Mrs. Lewis."

"Brian and I went to John Jay College together. He stopped in the restaurant a few weeks back. And—" she grinned "—we were planning our first date for tomorrow." She turned to Brian. "What are you doing here?"

Oh, my God, Elizabeth thought.

"I heard great things about the place and wanted to check it out." He patted his very flat stomach. "I could always use some exercise."

"Well, I've got to run. Desi is going to kill me," she said to her mother. She looked up at Brian. "I will leave you in my mother's very capable hands. Call me. We'll decide about tomorrow?"

"Tonight," Brian said.

She finger waved and ran out.

Brian turned to Elizabeth. "I know what you're thinking," Brian began, "but I had no idea she was your daughter. We hadn't gotten close enough to get into our family histories," he explained.

Elizabeth felt ill. She couldn't speak. Slowly, she returned to the desk and sat down. She lifted her head to look at him. "You can't continue to see her... Start to see her," she stammered. "There has to be some kind of ethical violation or some code you'd be breaking or something..." Elizabeth said as she felt hysteria bubbling in her stomach.

"I'm sure there is. But I have a problem and so do you. I like Dawne and I want to get to know her better. But, if I do get to know her, that might cause a conflict of interest if your business comes under investigation. And, if I continue to see her, that might mean that I would have to step away from this investigation. That's where the trouble comes in. Whether you believe it or not, I'm your ally. If I'm out of the picture, I'm sure you are going to get someone whose main goal in life is to make Ron Powers's and your lives miserable... someone like my partner, or someone worse."

Elizabeth blew out a ragged breath.

"I came to tell you, off the record, that, for the time being, no warrant is being issued. It seems that they can't find enough evidence to support one. And I also came to advise you to be sure that all of your papers and your documents are in order in the event that a warrant is issued."

"Why are you telling me this?"

He looked directly at her. "I didn't." With that he turned and walked out of the spa.

Chapter 12

There was only one highlight to the day that Elizabeth could fathom and that was that Sterling had found nothing unusual in the documents. He was going to have his assistant come in and do a thorough read, but, at least, on the surface, everything appeared to be in order.

She didn't mention to anyone that Brian had come by and she certainly didn't mention that he planned on dating her daughter. Every time she thought about that her stomach started spinning. What in the world had she done in a former life to get herself in this predicament?

Elizabeth made the left turn onto Ron's street. As much as she wanted to see him, she dreaded it at the same time. There was a lot that both of them were dealing with at the moment, they were vulnerable and tensions were high. She just hoped that neither of them said something they would regret later.

Surprisingly, she found a parking space. Had she arrived an hour later she might have been circling the block like a buzzard. Fortunately for her, most folks were still on their way home from work.

She locked the car door and walked up to his building. She used her key and let herself in the front door then headed for the elevator.

As much as he'd told her it was okay to use the key to his apartment, she still felt awkward. She rang the bell. Ron opened the door moments later.

"Hi. How come you didn't use your key?"

"Oh—" she screwed up her face "—I keep forgetting."

Ron stared at her. "No, you didn't," he said seeing right through her white lie. "Come on in."

She walked in front of him and into the apartment.

"You know, Ell, you're really beginning to scare me. If we can't be honest with each other about the little things, what's going to happen down the road?"

The impromptu visit by Brian Jennings leaped to mind. She ignored his question. He shut the door.

"Can I get you something?"

"No, thanks. I'm fine." She put her purse down on the couch and sat down.

"I'll get straight to it," Ron began. "I know I shouldn't have just walked out the other night without saying anything. But I really thought it was the best thing to do."

"Why? You were the one who said I should go to the hospital."

"I know. That was my gallant side, the humanitarian Ron, speaking. But then the man who's in love with you spoke up."

She felt her face grow warm.

"And I got scared," he said.

She searched his face with her eyes. "Of what?"

"Of the fact that you feel you have to hide things and lie to me when it comes to him…that this illness may be the thing that brings you back to him. And that, if something was to go on between the two of you, you wouldn't tell me."

She lowered her eyes, realizing that he was

edging very close to the truth. There was no way she could tell him about what she felt when she was with Matt, the things that went through her head, the memories, the feelings. She couldn't tell him because she was so unsure of it all herself.

"Would you?" he probed.

Her gaze jerked up. "Of course I would…but there's nothing to tell."

He came to stand in front of her and squatted down until they were at eye level. He stroked her cheek with the tip of his finger. "I don't believe you, baby. And I don't think you believe it, either."

She drew in a sharp breath of alarm. "Ron—"

He put his finger to her lips. "Shh," he said gently. "Listen to me. I want you to take the time you need to deal with Matt. I *need* you to take that time, Ell, 'cause I gotta know that, when you're with me, you're with *me*. I don't ever want you to wonder. Ya know?"

Her throat tightened until it hurt. Her eyes burned. He was telling her to go? Telling her to be with another man? Her gaze followed him in disbelief as he stood.

"Besides, with this cloud hanging over me, I don't need them checking any further because of my relationship with you." He pushed out a breath. "That's the way I see it, Ell. Best thing."

"So…it's over? Is that what you're telling me?"

His throat worked up and down for a moment. He glanced away then looked at her. "Yeah," he swallowed, "that's what I'm telling you."

Elizabeth felt like fine crystal that had just been dropped onto concrete, splintering into a million ragged pieces. But, if she was in a million pieces, she'd have to gather as much of herself and her dignity as she could and leave. Leave without falling apart further. Leave without him touching her and saying he was sorry he'd dropped her. Oh, God. Oh, God.

She blinked several times and blindly reached for her purse. Pushing herself to her feet, she drew in as much air as she could and walked to the door.

"Ell…"

Elizabeth turned the knob. If she looked at him, she knew she would fall apart. She opened the door and walked out.

Chapter 13

"Wonder where Ellie is," Barbara was saying to the "girlz" as she checked the clock.

"Yeah, I'm usually the last one to arrive," Stephanie said.

"Did she call?" Ann Marie asked.

"No, but she did say she needed to see Ron before she came here. So…" Her sentence hung in the air.

They all knew little bits and pieces about what was going on with Elizabeth's ex-husband, the issues surrounding Ron and how it was all twisted up together.

"Hey, maybe they kissed, made up and forgot all about us," Terri offered.

"I like the sound of that," Barbara said, "even if we will miss her being here."

Ann Marie brought out the chafing dish with the barbecue chicken and put it on the serving table next to the seasoned rice, green beans and potato salad.

"Sorry I didn't get to do too much," Barbara said, apologizing for the meager spread. Generally, at their get-togethers, they had two choices of meats, and a fish, two vegetables and a salad and at least two starches. Not to mention dessert.

"Barbara, please," Stephanie said, "there's plenty. We usually have too much." She put on a pretty pout. "So what, if there won't be any for me to take home."

The ladies laughed. Stephanie was notorious for her bad or rather nonexistent cooking. She was the main one who loaded up the Tupperware after one of their soirees.

"Try to save the poor chile' some leftovers," Ann Marie crowed. "We don't want that little baby she's carrying to starve."

"Yeah, Steph," Barbara said, dropping a spoonful of green beans on her plate. "You're really going to have to buckle down on your cooking skills. You can't eat out every night. It's not good for the baby."

Stephanie wrinkled her nose. "Tony is a great cook. I'd eat his cooking any day. Which I generally do." She chuckled.

"Hey, Steph, maybe me and you can take a cooking class," Terri said. "I can't cook worth a damn, either."

"If I must," Stephanie said with a dramatic sigh, and flopped onto the chair.

The doorbell rang. "That must be Ellie," Barbara said, heading to the door.

The instant Barbara pulled the door open, she knew something was wrong.

"Sorry I'm late," Elizabeth murmured, and walked inside, her gaze never making contact with Barbara.

"Honey, what's wrong?" Barbara closed the door and followed her inside.

The light banter stopped when Elizabeth walked into the room. All eyes zeroed in on her.

She barely spoke but went over to the serving table and began filling her plate. They all looked at each other with wide-eyed concern. And then they heard her soft sobs.

Barbara was the first one at her side. "Ellie,

what is it?" she asked, and put her arm around Elizabeth's shoulders.

"It's over," she said on a ragged breath. She wiped her eyes with a napkin.

"What's over? What are you talking about?"

"Me and Ron. It's over."

Barbara took the plate from Elizabeth's shaky hands. "Come and sit down." She guided her over to the couch and all her friends gathered around.

"What happened?" Stephanie asked.

"He said it's best that we 'take some time' until everything is settled with Matt."

They all knew what "take some time" meant—they'd all been there and done that.

Murmurs of understanding fluttered in the air.

"Why would he tell you something like that out of the blue?" Terri asked, not privy to all the details.

Elizabeth sniffed and wiped her eyes. "He thinks I'm still in love with my ex-husband."

"Oh…"

"Well, are you?" Ann Marie asked, always direct and to the point.

"That's just it, I don't know. I thought it was all over between us, you know? The divorce was final. I'd moved on and he'd moved on and then…" She told them all of the events of the past few days, Matt's diagnosis, the note that Ron found in her kitchen, everything leading up to Ron's declaration.

"Well, did you tell him it wasn't true?" Ann Marie asked.

"Not really."

Ann Marie huffed. "Well, what da 'ell ya think was going to 'appen?" she blasted, getting agitated. As usual, her accent was more pronounced when she became excited or upset.

"Men can't read between no lines, girl! Ya got to talk to dem straight or they get confused."

The ladies didn't want to laugh, but they knew exactly what Ann Marie meant.

"Are you still in love with Matt?" Stephanie asked gently.

"I don't know what I feel. I don't know if it's love, if it's concern, fear for him or just a lot of old feelings that I never dealt with."

"Well, you need to deal with it, Ellie," Barbara said, "for yourself and everyone concerned."

"Sometimes, after the dust settles, the past doesn't look so bad, anymore," Stephanie said, "and we forget what made us leave in the first place."

Elizabeth's gaze connected with Stephanie's.

That much was true, she thought. Matt's abandonment no longer hurt as much as it did. And, over time, although she knew that Matt betrayed her in the worst possible way, she'd begun to remember the good times between them, all the years they'd lived, loved and worked together. Had Matt not been so adamant about leaving her and their marriage, she knew she would have tried to work through it. But it didn't happen that way. She was a divorced woman—a divorced women with doubts.

"I don't know what to do," she finally said.

"Maybe, as hard as it is, you should take Ron's advice and take some time, Ellie," Terri said. "'Cause it really sounds like you are uncertain. You have too many emotions and misgivings going on right now to make a clear decision about anything."

"One of the few things I remember my mama telling me as a girl was, if you have two choices, line them up side by side, da good and da bad, and be honest," Ann Marie said. "After you make your list of good and bad for each, you'll see which one is best for you."

Elizabeth offered a crooked grin. "What if they come out equal?"

"Den, ya got yourself in one helluva jam."

* * *

Ron walked into the dimly lit bar on Amsterdam and 122nd Street. The raucous laughter from the clientele greeted him at the door. Boos and cheers were directed at the huge television screens around the space. It was just what he needed. After Ellie'd left, he didn't want to be alone with his thoughts so he'd called Ali and asked if he wanted to hang out for a while. Ali had agreed. They decided to meet at the local sports bar and restaurant to watch the Knicks game.

He peered inside and spotted Ali at a table in the back. He wound his way around the circular and rectangle tables until he reached him.

"Hey, man," Ali greeted, "you look like you just got your teeth kicked in."

Ron lowered himself onto the hard wooden seat. "Feel like it."

The waitress approached. "What can I get you?"

Ron looked up. "Beer for me."

"Same," Ali said.

"Thought you didn't drink."

"I don't. But the shape you're in I don't want you drinking alone." He chuckled good naturedly. He lifted his chin toward the television. "Knicks losing again," he groused, and shook his head.

"What else is new?"

They watched the game until their drinks arrived.

Ali raised his mug. "To things getting a helluva lot better and quick."

Ron raised his mug. "Got that right."

They took long swallows.

"So, you wanna tell me what's going on?"

"Broke up with Ellie."

"Not over this investigation bs?"

He shook his head. "That was part of it, but it's really about her husband."

"Husband?" His thick brows rose in alarm. "I thought she was divorced."

"She is."

"Oh." He let out a breath of relief. "Scared me there for a minute. But I still don't get it."

Ron explained the events that had transpired and how he felt that Elizabeth wasn't being straight with him or herself. "So I let her go."

Ali leaned back in his seat and folded his arms across his broad chest. "Man, are you crazy?"

"Huh?"

"Deaf, too? You don't turn your woman over to another man. Those ain't the rules." He leaned forward and rested his arms on the table. "Man, love is like…the Knicks."

"What?"

"This is the way I see it: The Knicks are a good team. They fight hard all the way through the game until the fourth quarter thinking they got the game in the bag. Then they let their guard down and, little by little, the opponent whittles away all the points until the last two minutes of the game. Now it's a struggle. They have to use all their best plays if they want to win. Down by two, with less than ten seconds to go. Coach says to go with their best three-point man. Game is in his hands." He paused and looked directly in Ron's eyes. "You're the three-point man. Either you're gonna go for it and win the game, or you're gonna shoot and miss." He tossed up his hands. "It's on you."

"Sounds real simple."

"It is. You're up against a team with a lot of years of experience." His mouth inched into a half smile.

"Maybe you're right."

"Of course I am." He finished off his beer. "Watch the game, brotha, and you'll see for yourself."

Several hours and a few beers later, Ron put the key into the door of his apartment. Something wasn't right. He felt it the instant he stepped inside. Quietly, he shut the door and eased inside.

There was a light coming from beneath the door of his bedroom. He took the bat he kept behind the door. If anything was to go down it wouldn't be easy. He approached his bedroom and pushed the door open, the bat gripped tightly in his fist.

"Ellie! What the hell…"

"I finally decided to use my key."

Chapter 14

Ron slowly approached her. "You could have gotten yourself hurt," he said, not knowing what else to say.

"Not as much as if I didn't come."

"What are you telling me?"

She stood and walked up to him. "I'm telling you that I'm in love with you, Ron Powers. Without doubt, without question. What I want to know is, do you feel the same way about me?"

His gaze slowly moved across her face. *Go for the point, or freeze.* "You know I do."

She reached up and caressed his cheek. "Then, we can work anything out. Anything."

"What about Matt?"

She breathed heavily. "I'm going to be honest with you. I care about Matt. That much, I do know. I also know that he's going through a really tough time now and he is depending on me to see him through it." She turned away and walked to the other side of the room and sat in the chair next to the bed. "And I will. I want you to know that." She slowly shook her head. "But nothing more than that. I know the kind of person I am, the kind of person you fell in love with. I couldn't live with myself if I turned my back on him. Not now. And I'm hoping that you will understand and accept that."

Ron's jaw clenched. He nodded his head. "All right," he finally said, "but no more secrets, Ell. No more sneaking around. If we are going to get through this we gotta be up front."

"I know. That was my mistake. My mistake in not trusting you enough to believe that you would understand."

He leaned against the dresser. "I guess those male hormones kicked in. I've been jealous as hell."

She smiled softly. "You have nothing to be jealous of. I promise you that."

His expression turned serious. "But we still have the investigation to deal with. Your association with me—"

She got up. "I talked to Barbara, Ann, Stephanie and Terri about it. We can handle it. You've done nothing wrong and neither have we."

"Are you sure?"

She walked closer. "Positive," she whispered. "Come here."

She stepped into his embrace, pressing her head against his chest as he wrapped his arms tightly around her. He stroked her hair and let his hands travel down her spin.

He really loved her, he thought. Loved her enough to let her go if need be; whatever it took to make her happy. He never thought he would feel that way about a woman. But he did.

He lowered his head and kissed her softly. She laced her fingers behind his head and pulled him deeply into the kiss. She felt his heart pound against her chest.

Ron reluctantly leaned back. "I'm going to get into the shower. I've been in these dusty clothes and body all day."

"Want some company?" she asked coyly.

His eyes darkened. "Absolutely."

She followed him into the small bathroom and

while he adjusted the temperature for the shower, she got undressed. When he turned around, she was just stepping out of her thong. She stood, and the heat from his eyes made the hair on the back of her neck stand on end.

His gaze ran up and down her body. "You're so beautiful," he said in awe, as if seeing her for the first time. He took the short step over to her and let his finger trail along her delicate collarbone. Elizabeth's body shuddered. His hand wandered down to the swell of her left breast, his thumb teased her nipple until it rose and hardened. He lowered his head and took it into his mouth.

Elizabeth moaned in delight. Her eyes drifted closed. She held his head to her, wanting him to take more, and he did. His hands cupped her waist as he suckled her, the act turning him on as much as it did her.

She needed to feel him, to press her body fully against his. She lifted his head from her breast and took his mouth, her tongue darting into his.

Ron pulled her tight against him, her naked body flush against the roughness of his T-shirt and jeans, the friction of the fabrics on her bare skin made her tingle with longing.

She grabbed the bottom of his shirt and tugged it over his head, practically ripping it in the process. Ron tossed it to the floor and took her mouth again as he undid his pants. Elizabeth pushed his hands away. He was taking too long. She unfastened him, pushed his jeans down over his hips and his erection pushed through his shorts. She didn't bother with them. She took him in her hand and stroked him.

His groans filled the room. He leaned back against the sink as her silky fingers traveled up and down the length of him. He gritted his teeth, holding back. He desperately needed her. Her finger brushed across the tender head and he swore he would explode right in her hand. But then he shot right to heaven when her mouth enveloped him.

"Ah, Ell…"

The room filled with steam.

She took him slow and easy, mimicking with her mouth what her hands had done. It was an awesome sense of power she experienced. Every muscle, every vein that jerked and pulsed she could feel. It was incredible.

"Ell," he groaned. He pulled at her head. "Ell…enough…you gotta stop, baby…"

Her eyes rolled up to look at him and what she saw was pure bliss. He looked down at her, a slow wicked grin, the kind that should only be seen after dark, moved across his mouth. "You are a very, very bad girl."

"Being bad feels so good," she cooed.

He pulled her up to him and, in one smooth motion, turned her around, her back to him. He bent her forward to lean on the sink.

"I want you," he hissed in her ear. "You do understand that," he said, and pushed up inside her.

"Ooh, yes," she cried out.

He arched his body back and held her hips in a death grip as he pumped in and out of her, slow and long and hard. She was so hot inside, so wet, so tight. It was as if he'd stepped outside of himself, the experience so intense he felt delirious with feeling—everywhere.

Elizabeth moaned out his name as she gripped the sink and rotated her hips. She wanted all of him, every inch. She couldn't seem to get enough.

And then he did something she'd only seen in an X-rated video. He lifted her by her hips and forced her legs around his back. He was holding her in midair, the only thing keeping her from falling was her hold on the sink and his arms wrapped around her waist. She locked her legs and he pushed and pushed. The sensation was surreal. With each thrust, her swollen clit got teased. Her body trembled. Ron pumped faster. His sweat dripped onto her back. Her muscles screamed. The heat from the steam enveloped them. She heard his ragged breathing in her ear.

"Ellie!" He grabbed her right breast and squeezed.

His rock solid erection throbbed inside her, hit that spot and her body imploded. She lost all control as wave after wave of electricity rushed through her. Her mouth opened to scream but nothing emerged.

"I love you, baby…love you," Ron moaned as the last of him filled her.

With great effort, Elizabeth dropped her legs to the floor and slid down to the cool, damp tiles. Ron collapsed next to her and pulled her against his chest. His heart was still racing.

"Guess we're not as old as we thought," he said, a bit breathless.

She looked at him with a silly grin on her face. "Forget the shower, we need a hot soak."

Ron reached over to the tub and put the stopper in the drain. The water from the shower slowly filled the tub. Standing, he then leaned down and lifted her into his muscular arms and lowered her into the steamy water. She closed her eyes and sighed contentedly. He stepped into the tub behind her and pulled her close, wrapping his arms around her. He kissed the back of her neck then cupped her breasts in his palms, massaging them gently.

"Hmm." She sighed. "It doesn't get better than this."

He thought about his conversation with Ali and was glad he'd taken the three-pointer.

"Just so you know," Elizabeth said the following morning, while she hunted around for her discarded clothing, "I'm going to meet with Matt later today. I'd put off calling him. But I know he wants to talk about his decision for his treatment. And we need to tell our daughters what's going on."

"You haven't told them yet?"

She shook her head.

"You gotta do that, Ell. Even if he won't, you need to."

"I know." She put on her recovered underwear. "I plan on seeing them later on today." She hesitated a moment. "There's something else I need to tell you."

He stopped stripping the bed and turned to

her. He couldn't imagine any more surprises. "What?"

"That FBI guy…"

"Yeah…"

"He's seeing Dawne."

She told him about Brian coming to the spa and Dawne showing up. "I couldn't have been more stunned. I haven't told anyone—except you."

"Geez, what next?"

"Don't even ask," she said drolly. "At some point, all of this has to come to a grinding halt."

"Well, I have to agree with you on this one. Just leave it alone. We definitely don't want to push that Jennings the wrong way."

"He seemed truly sincere, ya know—about Dawne."

"He's in a pretty awkward spot, himself."

"Exactly." She finished dressing.

"There's not much we can do but wait it out."

"I agree." She went up to him and kissed him tenderly. "Thank you for understanding…about Matt. We're going to get through this."

"From your mouth…"

She pecked him one last time. "I gotta run. I have a full day. I'll call you as soon as I can." She grabbed her bag and headed for the door.

Ron sat down on the side of the bed. Well, he'd taken his shot, now he had to wait and see if he was going to be fouled.

Kate sat down on the edge of the bed, with
a dazed lo... on her face. It was all too much...
if he wasn't going to be...

Chapter 15

Barbara was thankful for a day off, from the spa
and work. She needed some time to herself.

The conversations the ladies had the night before didn't really hit her until after they were
gone. All of them were experiencing difficult issues and choices in their relationships.

Stephanie had to deal with the fact that Tony
had a daughter who would become a part of
their lives. Ann Marie had finally broken free of
the emotional hold that her former husband, Terrance, had on her to be able to make a life with
Sterling. Ellie had come to terms with the idea

that you can't go back and that Ron was her future. Even Terri had given up her career because she knew that her love for Michael was more important.

On the surface, these were the types of situations that would make women activists cringe—women sacrificing all for the men they loved. But, Barbara realized the issues were so much deeper than that.

Love and happiness brought fulfillment in a way that a job, a new house, friends and even a fabulous career never could. It pushed the darkness away and brought light into your life. Her client, Veronica, was a perfect example of the power of love and, now, so were her girlfriends.

She put the remainder of the dishes in the dishwasher and turned it on, straightened up the living room then washed down the bathroom and collected the dirty clothes for the laundry.

The only one left at the crossroads was her, she realized as she poured her second cup of tea for the morning.

Barbara went to stand by her living room window. She looked down the six stories to the hustle and bustle below. New York had been her home for years. It was where she and her husband, Marvin, had decided to build their lives.

Although they'd never been blessed with children, they'd had a good life here.

She sighed, and thought about her short but thrilling affair with Michael. He, too, had suggested that she leave, follow him. It had been tempting, but she'd balked then, as well. As it turned out, it had been for the best. But, at the time, when she'd been undecided about a move with Michael, she had been for the same reasons she was now—her life, her job, her friends, her business were here in New York.

She thought again about Veronica's words of wisdom. Sure, she would miss her friends, someone would fill her job and the big, bad Apple wouldn't miss one less person. So, what was holding her back from telling Wil that she would love to go with him to North Carolina and build a new life?

Fear. Plain and simple. Fear of the unknown. Everything around her was familiar. She'd become so entrenched that she couldn't lift her feet out of the sludge. But the risk of staying in place was that you never moved forward and life would simply pass you by.

The beep of the dishwasher gently shook her from her thoughts. *So what is it going to be,*

Babs? Her heart knocked in her chest. Oh, how easy it was to simply sit on the fence. She smiled ruefully and turned away from the window.

"I'm coming over," Elizabeth said into the phone. "I should be there in about a half hour. We need to talk, Matt, and we need to decide what to tell the girls."

"Fine. I'll be here waiting."

Elizabeth hung up the phone. She was determined to set the parameters straight between her and Matt, once and for all. He wasn't going to use guilt to get her to give up and give in. She wanted to be there for him, but she also had a responsibility to herself and her relationship with Ron.

Elizabeth made a last minute check that everything was in order in her apartment, stopped downstairs at the spa and made sure that there was no crisis that couldn't wait then hurried out to her car. The sooner she got this over with, the better she would feel. The reality was, as hard as it was to swallow, her and Matt wouldn't be in this situation if he hadn't cheated on her. She kept that thought at the forefront of her mind as she pressed the buzzer to his apartment.

"Glad you came, Ell," he said, and stepped aside to let her in.

"How are you feeling?"

"Not bad, actually. The change in meds helped. The doctor said, as soon as I'm finished with the antibiotics…he wants me to get started with treatment."

She walked into the apartment, still amazed by the stylish splendor. She took a seat in one of the armchairs.

"You're looking pretty businesslike today," he said, attempting to lighten the mood.

"I'm going to get right to the point—"

He held up his hand. "I know the whole thing about ladies first, but there's something I need to tell you. Something I should have told you a long time ago." He drew in a breath. "I knew something was wrong while we were married."

Her eyes widened. "What are you talking about?"

"At first, I figured I was just tired, overworked. I didn't want you to know that I couldn't… perform… at least, not how I used to. So I stopped making love to you. I wanted to blame you somehow, make myself believe that I was no longer attracted to you and that's why I couldn't…" He swallowed and looked away. "That's why I took up with…her. I wanted to prove something to myself, convince myself that it was because I didn't love you, anymore, that I couldn't perform."

Her body grew tense. She couldn't believe what she was hearing.

"At first I was fine. And I figured I was right, that the love and desire was gone. But I was wrong, Ell. That wasn't what was wrong with me. I just refused to face it. Refused to go see my doctor. I was scared. Scared to face my fears and I sacrificed our marriage in the process."

Elizabeth didn't know if she wanted to scream in rage or burst out in tears of anguish. Her stomach rolled until it knotted into a tight ball of fire.

She stared at him in disbelief. He ruined their marriage, damaged her emotions beyond repair, disrupted their family all because he was afraid of his own immortality.

"I know I should have told you…"

"Don't," she said, finally finding her voice. "Don't try to explain it away." She lowered her head, fought back tears. She looked across at him. "I wish," she said slowly, "that what you said could make everything go away, Matt." She drew in a breath. "But it can't. Our marriage was built on trust and honoring each other. You violated both of those things. You didn't trust me enough to tell me what you *thought* was wrong. Instead, you made me *think* it was me, that I had done something to deserve your coldness. Do you have any idea what that did to me?"

"Ell—"

"You dishonored our marriage and the vows we spoke when you slept with another woman— whatever your reason. In sickness and in health, Matt. In sickness and in health. That's what we said, it's what we promised each other."

Slowly, almost painfully, she stood. His eyes rose to meet hers as she did.

"I'm sorry, Ellie. I swear to you, I'm sorry."

"I know," she said gently. "So am I." She wiped at her eyes. "I'll always love you, Matt, but not in the way you want and not in the way you need." She shook her head. "We can't go back and undo everything. I'm going to move on with my life and you have to, as well. And I won't let you use this illness to guilt me into coming back. That, I won't do. So you need to decide about your treatment and I plan to tell the girls. They'll be there for you like I will. You don't need to do this alone."

He hung his head. "I understand." He looked up at her, realizing all that he'd lost.

She pressed her lips together into a tight line of sadness then turned and walked out.

Elizabeth returned to her car and for a long time she simply sat still. She'd made a decision back there that would forever seal their future. It hurt, deeply, There was no denying how bad it hurt. But, as sad as it was to admit, she felt oddly relieved. She knew she'd given her all to her marriage, to her husband and to her children, often at the expense of herself.

For months, she'd berated herself, belittled her womanhood, believing that somehow it had been her fault, that she had sent her husband into the arms of another woman. It wasn't her. It was fear and mistrust. Fear and mistrust had destroyed her marriage. It was eroding a country. It was a powerful, insidious weapon.

But she wouldn't let the effects of it dictate her actions or make her second-guess herself any longer. She put the car in gear and drove away.

Matthew would be all right and so would she. She headed to her daughters' restaurant. They needed to talk.

By the time she reached *Delectables* it was the height of the lunch-hour rush. Most of the tables were full and the counter seats were occupied from end to end. She pulled the door open and stepped inside and was welcomed by the aroma of something wonderful.

She spotted Dawne behind the counter and her twin, Desiree, in the back taking an order. She found an empty seat and waited. Perhaps this wasn't the best time, she thought, realizing how the news would upset them. But putting it off wouldn't lessen the burden.

Shortly, Dawne arrived at her table. "Mom." She leaned down and gave her a kiss. "This is a surprise."

Elizabeth smiled at her daughter while, at the same time, knowing that she was seeing the man who was trying to build a case against Ron. She shook off the thought. "Hey, sweetie. Busy, I see."

"Hmm, that's putting it mildly. Can I get you something or are you just hanging out?"

"What smells so good?"

Dawne's eyes brightened. "A new soup. You'll love it. I would tell you the ingredients but then I'd have to kill you." She grinned. "Want to try some?"

"Absolutely."

Dawne started to walk off. Elizabeth clasped her arm. "Honey, when you bring the soup back could you bring Desi with you. I need to talk to you both."

The happiness, which had been there seconds before, vanished. "What is it?"

"I want to tell you both at the same time. Okay."

"Ma, you're scaring me."

"Go get my soup and bring your sister."

Desiree arrived before the soup. "What's going on? Dawne said you wanted to talk to us."

Elizabeth looked over Desiree's shoulder and saw Dawne on her way with her order. She slid onto the booth next to her sister. She held on to the soup. "Talk first, eat later."

"Fine." Elizabeth drew in a long breath. "There's no easy way to say this so I'm just going to tell you. Your father is sick."

"Sick? Like what kind of sick?" Dawne asked.

"He has prostate cancer."

Both of them gasped in unison.

"Dad."

"Oh, no. How bad is it?"

"They caught it early, but not early enough. He has to have treatment."

"Chemo?" Desiree dared to ask.

"We don't know yet. Your father still has to decide on the course of action. He's been offered several options."

The twins were silent, letting the information sink in.

Dawne looked at her mother. "How long have you known?"

"A few days. He called me and wanted me to go with him to the hospital for the biopsy."

"I can't believe it," Desiree said in a far off voice. "Dad has always been so healthy." Her face drew into tight lines of worry. "Cancer."

"We need to go see him, Des," Dawne said.

Desiree nodded.

"There's something else you both need to know."

"You're not sick, are you?" Dawne asked, her voice rising in panic.

Elizabeth patted her hand. "I'm fine, sweetheart."

"So what is it?" Desiree asked.

Elizabeth cleared her throat. "The past year has been extremely difficult. What happened between me and your father hurt me deeply and I know that both of you hold him responsible for that. Today your dad told me all of the reasons why…" She explained to them as best she could about Matthew and his affair, how it happened and why. When she was finished they all had tears in their eyes.

"I hated him for what he did to you," Dawne said. "But I didn't know. I just thought he was being like all the men you read about who cheat on their wives. He was another statistic."

"It didn't have to happen," Desiree said, her voice empty.

"Now that you know…does this mean that you're going to give him another chance, try to work things out?" Dawne asked.

"I wish it was that easy, sweetheart."

"Does that mean, no?" Dawne asked in disbelief. "You can't walk out on him now." Her voice rose. "Not when you know why and all that he's going through."

"Dawne, it's much deeper than saying I'm sorry and brushing it off."

"No, it's not! He hurt you, yes, but he's sorry. He's sick and he did it because he was scared. Not because he didn't love you—didn't love *us*, anymore. This is about Ron, isn't it?" she threw at her mother.

"Dawne!"

"It is, isn't it? He put you up to this. Would you walk out on him, too, if he did something wrong?"

"D, chill," her sister admonished. "This is about Mom and Dad, not you. It's her decision and her life."

She glared at her sister, jumped up and stormed off. Moments later, she was out the door.

Elizabeth sat there transfixed. She couldn't believe what had just happened. Her daughters had been her greatest supporters during the months of separation and the subsequent divorce. They were the ones who pushed her into going out again, giving Ron a chance; Dawne, in particular.

"She'll come around. She just needs to come to grips with it, that's all," Desiree said, hoping to ease the distraught look on her mother's face.

"What about you?"

"It's hard to accept the fact that Dad could be such a screw up. He was always my knight in shining armor and could do no wrong, ya know? The whole thing is a rude awakening and now to find out why…" She shook her head sadly and looked at her mother. "Dad will get through it. Me and Dawne will make sure of that and so will you. In the meantime, you have your own life to live, Mom. Dad made a choice and, unfortunately, he has to live with the consequences. You can't expect to hurt people and destroy lives and not have to pay for it in some way."

"When did you get so wise?"

Desiree grinned. "Must be all this health food." She clasped her mother's hand. "Or good genes," she said with affection. "I'll talk to Dawne when she calms down. Okay. So don't worry about her. She's the hothead, I'm the cute one, remember?"

Elizabeth laughed. "Don't tell her that." She pulled her bowl of soup toward her. "I know you need to get back to your customers but I wanted to ask you something."

"Sure."

"The other day, Dawne's friend, Brian, came to the spa."

Desiree's brows rose in surprise. "Really. That's great. What about him?"

"Well, Dawne was there and I indirectly found out that they plan on seeing each other."

Desiree shrugged. "Okay, is there a question in this somewhere?"

"You've obviously been around him more than I have. What do you think of him."

Desiree twisted her lips to the side in thought. "The first couple of times when he came in I thought he was cute, just kind of uptight, if you know what I mean—like his collar was too tight or something. He started talking to D or, rather, *she* started talking to him— She's the aggressive one." Desiree winked at her mother. "I don't know, I guess they kind of like each other. He seems nice enough and he's smart enough to know the difference between the two of us. So he gets major points for that." She wrinkled her brow. "Why?"

"Just wondering. I hadn't heard anything about him."

Desiree took the bowl of soup from her mother. "Let me get you a fresh bowl. You really can't appreciate the flavors when it starts getting cold."

Elizabeth watched her daughter bounce away. Hmmph, nice guy and FBI agent was an oxymoron. Of all the people in the world for her daughter to get involved with. She certainly couldn't say anything to Dawne now, not after her declaration about her father and believing that Ron was at the root of her refusal to go back to Matthew. Any mention of Brian investigating Ron would only reinforce any misgivings Dawne may have.

She turned to look out the plate-glass window. If there was any justice in the world, Brian would turn out to be one of the good guys and leave *her* good guy alone.

Chapter 16

Stephanie was dragging her feet today. She couldn't seem to get herself together. Each time she stood up her head spun and her stomach revolted.

"Arrgh, I can't take it," she wailed, and flopped back down on the bed.

Tony stood over her with a cup of tea and some crackers. "Here, baby, try to get this down. I called the doctor and he said it would help."

"Baby, baby, that's the problem," she groaned, and shut her eyes. "All along, I've been fine. Now I just want to die. How am I going to get through two more months of this? Oh, Lord, suppose this morning sickness lasts through my entire pregnancy?"

Tony tried not to panic, she sounded utterly miserable. "It won't."

"How would you know? Have you ever been pregnant?" she snapped.

The question was like a punch in the gut. No he hadn't, but Kim had. And every day that she was, all he could do was pray for one more day with her.

When he found out that Stephanie was pregnant he felt a mixture of elation and fear. Kim's pregnancy had killed her and, to this day, years later, the guilt still rested quietly in his soul.

Stephanie reached up and grabbed his hand. "I'm sorry," she whispered seeing the pained look on his face. "That was totally insensitive of me."

He blinked the images away. "It's okay. I know you didn't mean it that way." He gazed down at her. "If anything ever happened to you…" His voice caught.

"Nothing is going to happen to me except that I'm going to get fat and grumpy." She smiled and let her eyes drift across his face.

"Hmm, I think I'll love you, anyway."

She poked him in the arm. "You betta." She pushed herself to a sitting position on the bed. At least the room didn't move. "There's something we need to talk about."

"Sure."

"I know that your sister, Leslie, has been taking care of your daughter, Joy. And I'm sure Joy is happy, but now with our baby coming I think we need to start making plans for Joy to come and live with us."

"I'd been thinking the same thing. I just wasn't sure when."

"It would be great if she could be here during the whole pregnancy so that she would feel a part of everything."

"Couple of problems."

"What?"

"Although both of us have really jazzy apartments, neither one is big enough for both of us, Joy and a baby."

"Which brings me to my next point."

"And that is?"

"We need to buy a house. If we're going to be a family, then we need a family house. I want *our* kids to have room to stretch out, a backyard, run up and down the stairs, not the elevator."

"Are you thinking of leaving Manhattan?"

"Unless we can find something here with a reasonable sized yard in back. Let's be honest, I can do PR from anywhere. You don't have to be locked in a space to do your photography and graphics. That's why they invented the Internet." She winked.

He playfully popped her on the nose. "Smarty."

"But, seriously, if we have to leave, I don't mind." She took his hand. "As long as all of us are together."

"If we leave New York, or at least the city, what about your sister, Samantha."

She drew in a breath. "That was the other thing. I want to bring Sam with us."

Tony's dark brown eyes widened. "Are you serious?"

"Very. She's making tremendous progress. She'll never be one hundred percent, I know that, but I want to be near her."

"It's a lot of responsibility, baby. Me, Joy, a new baby and Sam. I mean, I know you can bring home the bacon fry it up in a pan and all, but…"

She whacked him again on the arm. "Very funny."

"You must be feeling better, your right hook is stronger." He chuckled. She made a face.

"Babe, whatever you want to do, we'll make it work. I'm along for the ride."

"Are you sure?"

"As sure as you are."

Damn, she loved this man. "Then, we need to start making some real plans, huh?" She squeezed his hand.

"Yeah, I think we do."

Never one to spend time wasting time, Stephanie got herself in gear while Tony was in the shower. By the time he got out and was dressed, she'd booked an appointment with Ann Marie to go house hunting.

"Are you sure you're up for this?" Tony asked as he tucked his shirt in his pants.

"Well, if morning sickness holds true to its name, I'm done until tomorrow." She turned from side to side in the mirror trying to imagine her slender figure rounded. At least, she finally got some breasts to go along with her behind.

"You look beautiful," he said, sliding his arms around her waist. He lifted her hair from her shoulders and tenderly kissed the back of her neck.

She turned in his arms to face him. "In a couple of months, you won't be able to get this close," she whispered, and brushed her lips against his.

He ran his hand down her back and pulled her closer. "You mean, like this?"

"Hmm. Yeah, like this," she murmured against his mouth.

"What time do we have to meet Ann Marie?"

"An hour."

He began unbuttoning her blouse. "I can get us there in five minutes."

She giggled as they tumbled onto the bed.

"Know what I've been thinking?" Tony said as he moved slowly inside her.

"That this is the best love you've ever made?" She rolled her hips against him.

"That, too. But I was thinking that I don't want to move into a house with my baby's mama."

She froze. "What?"

He braced his weight above her and looked down into her eyes. "I want to move into a home with my wife."

Her heart thumped in her chest. "What are you saying?"

"I want to marry you, Steph. Make a life with you and our children. I want to take care of you for as long as there is a breath in my body."

"Tony?" she said, breathless.

"Marry me, Stephanie Moore, be my wife, my soul mate."

She couldn't find words. They were stuck somewhere between fear and terror. A baby she could deal with, a five-year-old child she could open her heart to, a boyfriend she could enjoy— A husband? It was so final, so permanent, so real. A wife?

"On one condition," she said.

"Anything."

"That you promise to love me just like this for as long as we both shall live."

A smile as bright as daybreak spread across his face. "It's a tough job…but somebody's got to do it."

She wrapped her arms around him and opened herself up to all that he offered, everything that he promised. Maybe after house-hunting they could go diamond-ring shopping! Wait til she told the girls.

Barbara was just getting ready to run a few errands when her phone rang. She did an about-face and picked up the extension in the kitchen.

"Chile', guess what?"

"I haven't got a clue, Ann Marie." She put down her bag of laundry.

"Well, I'll tell ya. Stephanie and Tony just made an appointment with me to look at houses."

"Get out of here."

"Ya heard me right."

"Wow."

"Looks like our girl is really going to settle down. I still can't believe that this is the same woman who, just a year ago, was messing around with her married boss."

"Finding the right man can change your mind about a lot of things," Barbara said as realization slowly dawned on her.

Chapter 17

Matthew hadn't moved from the couch since Elizabeth left earlier in the day. Were it not for the full moon he would've been wrapped in total darkness. Long shadows stretched out across the floor. He'd never felt more alone.

Throughout the months, there had been a part of him that held on to the hope that Elizabeth would come back to him. He'd been so sure that, after he finally told her about his health, she would come running. She had, but not in the way he wanted.

Ellie had been his first and only love. From the

moment he saw her all those years ago, he knew
that she was the one for him. They'd had a good
marriage, one that others wanted to duplicate.

Getting involved with Theresa had been so
stupid. It was if some other person had gotten
into his head. He'd wanted to prove his manhood
and Theresa had provided the vehicle. She'd
made it easy.

They'd been working together for about four
years. She was bright, eager, talented and pretty.
She'd always been willing to help out on projects,
go the extra mile. He knew he could depend on
her.

They were working late one evening and his
car was in the shop for some minor repairs. Theresa had offered to drop him off at the train station.

"It's not a problem, Matt," she'd said. "It's pouring outside. I can drive you home if you want."

The prospect of hiking through the downpour wasn't in the least bit appealing. "You're
on," he'd said. "Let me get my coat and I'll be
right with you."

"How's your wife and your daughters," Theresa had asked as they'd darted to her car beneath
Matthew's umbrella.

"Good. Have to get you back over for dinner
sometime."

"I'd like that. Your daughters are so much fun."

Matthew chuckled.

Theresa opened the door to her ten-year-old Honda Accord.

"It looks a mess but it drives like a dream," she said, referring to the dents and dings and duck tape around the fender.

"I hope you didn't cause all of these."

She got inside, and Matt slid into his seat.

"Whew." She leaned over and stuck the key in the ignition. "No. My brother. Every time I loan him my car, some 'mystery driver' bumps into him."

"Younger or older?"

"Older. You would think he'd know better or at least have his own car." She laughed. "He's a pain, but I love him. What about you, any brothers or sisters?"

"No. Only child."

"Wow. So you must have been a spoiled brat, huh?"

"Actually, pretty much the opposite. If anything went missing or got broken I had no one to blame."

There was that infectious laugh again. "Yeah, that's true."

"Hey, you just went past the train station."

"I know. I figured I may as well drive you home. It's no big deal, really."

"I owe you," he said.

"Lunch."

"Deal."

Had it begun then? he wondered, staring out into the night. Or when she'd told him they'd known each other long enough that she could call her Terri—all her friends did. Too many nights, he'd asked himself, at what moment did he mentally cross the line into adultery? It starts there, in your head—the thoughts and images take hold and begin to take on a life of their own.

Or did it start when he was in bed with his wife and couldn't perform, and not for the first time? It was intermittent at first, so he passed it off as exhaustion. But that wasn't it, there were other symptoms that he'd refused to address. Instead, he'd let the images take over, give him an excuse, somewhere to put blame. If he could blame his adultery on Elizabeth, somehow he could escape his guilt and avoid a truth he refused to accept— that he was sick. But if he didn't acknowledge it, if he didn't confirm it, then it wasn't real.

He snorted at his stupidity. How many television advertisements, billboards and posters had he seen urging men to get checked? But he'd convinced himself that it "could never be me." Sure, it ran in the family, but "not me. My problem is with my wife. My wife who can't satisfy me, anymore."

His ego, his false sense of male invincibility had destroyed his marriage.

In the distance he thought he heard the bell followed by knocking. Go away, he thought he said. But the knocking persisted.

He pulled himself up and went to the door. "Who is it?" he barely got out.

"Dad, it's me, Dawne. Open the door."

He shut his eyes and reluctantly opened the door.

"What took you so long? I've been ringing the downstairs bell for ten minutes. Finally, one of your neighbors came and let me in. Are you all right?"

"I'm fine."

"Can I come in?"

"I—I was resting."

"Dad, I want to talk to you."

"Not now, Dawne." He wouldn't move from in front of the door.

"Dad…I know. Mom told us today."

His entire body seemed to deflate. He turned away from her and walked back inside.

Dawne stepped into the darkness and shut the door behind her. As she followed him inside, she turned on the lights. When she looked at her father, her heart skipped a beat. He looked as if he'd aged ten years since she'd last seen him. His eyes were empty. He looked haggard. Her fear escalated.

She put down her bag and slowly sat. "Dad, talk to me, please."

"What do you want to talk about?"

"You. Your health. I want to hear it from you."

"I have cancer," he said simply.

"What are you doing? How are they going to treat it?"

"I haven't decided yet."

"Why not? Dad, you can't waste time. You can't."

"I thought it would be a decision your mother and I would make together but…"

"So, because of that, you're going to do nothing? I can't believe you. What about us?"

He dragged his gaze to meet hers.

"What about us, Dad? I know why you messed around on Mom and I hated you for that. Hated you for hurting her that way. She didn't deserve it. Now you want to punish us, too, by forcing us to watch you die—while you make a decision? When are you going to stop being so selfish?"

The words were like a cold bucket of water being doused on his head.

"I spent all afternoon at the library." She reached in her bag and took out a bunch of papers. "I got all the information I could find on treatments." She shoved them at him. "You're going to make a decision. And I'm not leaving here until you do." When he didn't react she put them on his lap then folded her arms in defiance. "I'm the aggressive one, Desiree is the cute one, remember? Read."

A sad smile drifted across his mouth. He knew that once Dawne got something into her head, that was it. He'd either come to a decision or she would sit there until the end of time.

"You're cute, too," he said, lifting the papers from his lap.

Dawne leaned back against the cushion of the chair. "That's what I keep telling Desi." She smiled at her father. "Read."

"You don't know how much this means to me you coming here, Dawne," he said as she puttered around in the kitchen preparing something to eat.

"I wasn't going to, at first," she admitted. She turned away from the counter and faced him.

"When Mom told us, I got so mad at her. I said some really ugly things."

"Why?"

She shrugged and sighed heavily. "I felt that she had an obligation to stand by you, to forgive you."

Matthew lifted his chin. "Your mom is a good one, Dawne. I don't want you to blame her for anything. I did enough of that. She has her own life now and she's entitled to live it."

She sat down at the counter. "I know. And I know I'm not some preteen who falls apart over the idea that her parents aren't together anymore. It's just…" She lowered her head.

Matthew reached across the table and covered her hand with his. "I know. It's not easy. Everyone hopes that their parents will stay together forever. Sometimes it just doesn't work out that way. We had a good marriage. I screwed that up. Not your mother. As hard as it is for me to admit, I do want her to be happy, even if it is with someone else. She deserves that."

"Ron is a real nice guy. I think you'd like him." Once the words were out of her mouth she couldn't believe she was talking to her father about another man in her mother's life.

"Do you?" he asked, biting into his sandwich.

"Yeah. He's cool."

Matthew nodded. "Maybe I'll get to meet him one day."

Dawne's brows rose. "Are we going to turn into one of those 'modern' families?"

Matthew chuckled. "Looks that way. Finish your sandwich so we can go over this stuff."

"I love you, Dad," she said softly.

"I know," came his gentle reply.

By the time Dawne left several hours later, he'd come to a decision about his treatment. First thing tomorrow, he was going to see Dr. Chavis.

On the drive home to her studio apartment in the West Village, Dawne thought about her visit with her father. She was glad that she went. She'd been irrationally angry at her mother and owed her an apology. She remembered, all too well, how hurt her mother had been, how devastated. Yes, her mother did deserve to be happy and, if she was happy with Ron, then so be it.

Her father's health crisis had been an awakening for all of them. Life was too short to hold resentments. She was letting hers go. Her entire belief in marriage had been shaken. When she'd looked at her parents, it made her believe in forever. But she couldn't build her life on the image of someone else. She had to do that on her own, which made her think of Brian.

She smiled. He was just the kind of guy she'd been looking for. He reminded her in many ways of her father; good-looking, hardworking, focused. She was definitely going to give it her all. She just hoped he didn't have any skeletons in his closet.

Chapter 18

He knew he should have never gone to the spa, unofficially. He should have never spoken to Mrs. Lewis. If it ever got out, the entire case, for what it was worth, would be compromised. But, in his estimation, it was going nowhere fast. Now he also had Dawne to consider. He wanted to get to know her. But what would she think if she found out that he was investigating her mother's boyfriend, or worse, what if his superiors found out about his involvement with her and her connections to the case?

The best thing to do was to wrap this up as

quickly as possible, clear this Powers guy and move on. But what if he couldn't?

His phone rang.

"Jennings."

"Hi, Brian. It's Dawne."

He turned his back to the opening of his cubicle and lowered his voice. "Hey, how are you?"

"Good. I was thinking about you and thought I'd call. Busy on some great mystery over there?" she teased.

"Yeah, something like that."

"Listen, I was just calling to confirm about tonight. We're still on, right?"

"Sure. I'll pick you up at seven."

"Great. At the restaurant. I won't have time to go home if we want to make the show."

"I'll be there."

"Looking forward to seeing you."

"Me, too," he said.

He slowly hung up the phone. At least, thinking about his first date with Dawne would hopefully make the day fly by.

"So, you ready for your big date with Brian tonight?" Desiree asked as they worked side by side in the kitchen preparing the ingredients for the house special—soup.

Dawne beamed. "Yeah. I'm excited. Haven't been on a real date in ages."

"That's cause you're too hard on men. You expect all of them to be like Dad."

"Is that so wrong? Dad is a good guy and he was my first love," she said in a feigned dreamy voice. "I went to see him last night."

Desiree stopped cutting the celery. "You did? And?"

"We had a long talk about a lot of things, the mistakes he made, his love for us and Mom. I felt really sorry for him. Mom was his whole world but he blew it and now he's regretting it. But…he did say he wants her to be happy, that's the most important thing to him. I owe Mom an apology. I was really ugly, yesterday."

"Who you telling? But she understands."

"I finally got him to decide on his treatment. He promised me that he was going to see his doctor today."

"Oh, thank goodness." She breathed a sigh of relief. "Mom will be relieved to hear that."

"I'll give her a call later."

"Good. Make sure that you do. So where are you and Brian going tonight?"

"We are going to The Comedy Club. We have reservations for the first show."

"That should be fun and not too demanding."

"Exactly. I thought about an intimate dinner, but I didn't want to put any pressure on him."

"You really like this guy, huh?"

She grinned. "Yeah. I mean, we haven't had a lot of time to get to know each other. Just talking here at the restaurant. But there's something about him that appeals to me."

"I hope it works out. He seems nice. What exactly does he do for the FBI, anyway? That always sounds so ominous to me."

"I know. He doesn't really say." She shrugged. "Guess it's top secret stuff— *His eyes only.*"

"You're silly." She added her ingredients to the simmering pot then wiped her hands on her apron. "I'm all done here. I'm going to check up front and see how things are going."

She thought about her sister's question regarding Brian and his job. It was a bit disconcerting not knowing what he did. Maybe she'd find a way to bring it up during the evening, see what he said.

The day flew by relatively quickly. Before she realized, it was already six o'clock. Brian would be arriving in an hour. She went to the back to the employees' rest room with her change of clothes and makeup bag. She applied fresh makeup and put on a brand-new pair of Apple Bottom jeans and an light pullover sweater, ran a comb through her hair and was ready.

When she came out front, she was surprised to see Ron and Ali sitting at a table in the back. Her one-sided argument with her mother the day before regarding Ron rushed to mind.

One of the new waitresses they'd recently hired was taking their order. She went over, anyway.

"Hello, guys," she greeted.

Ron looked up and smiled. "Hello, yourself."

"You're looking mighty nice. Hot date?"

She grinned. "Something like that."

Inwardly, Ron cringed and wondered if the hot date was with Agent Jennings. He didn't have to wait long to find out. The chimes over the door rang and Brian walked in.

He stopped short at the door when he saw Ron and Ali talking with Dawne but quickly recovered.

Dawne broke out in a grin and walked over to greet him.

"What the hell is going on?" Ali whispered.

"I'll tell you about it later. Just be cool."

Dawne walked over arm-in-arm with Brian. "Ron, Ali, this is my friend, Brian Jennings."

Ron held his breath wondering how this was going to go down.

Brian extended his hand to Ron, then Ali. "Nice to meet you both."

"Ron is a good friend of my mother's," Dawne said. "Actually, he was the contractor who worked on the spa."

"Really? I happened to stop by the other day. I'd heard so much about it." He focused on Ron. "Outstanding job."

"Thank you," he said.

"Well, we better get going," Dawne said to Brian.

"Yeah, don't want to be late." He turned his attention to the men at the table. "Good to meet you both."

"Uh, same here," Ali muttered. "What the hell was that?" he asked the instant they'd walked out the door.

"I should have told you. Apparently, Dawne and Mr. G-man went to school together. He stopped in the restaurant one day and they reconnected."

Ali ran his hand across his face. "Geez. What are the odds of that?"

"New York. Go figure."

"So what kind of game is he playing?"

"I have no idea. But, apparently—at least for the time being—he's gonna act like everything is cool."

Ali looked toward the door. "Yeah, for the time being."

"What ever made you decide to go into the FBI?" Dawne was asking during intermission at The Comedy Club.

He picked up his drink of rum and coke and took a thoughtful sip. "Well, obviously going to John Jay College for Criminal Justice had me thinking about law enforcement. I knew I didn't want to be an attorney and I didn't want the stress of being a cop on the street."

"Yes, that is definitely a job that takes more than heart to do every day. But, unfortunately, the climate for police on the street is at an all time low. With all the shootings of unarmed men, the profiling. It's just a bad time all around." She shook her head sadly.

"Exactly. Anyway, I think this was after you'd left John Jay, but there was a seminar and they brought in some speakers from the agency. I was impressed. But I was also taken by the lack of black agents. That's where I thought I could make a difference on an even broader scale than local law enforcement."

She nodded. "Hmm. Makes sense." She glanced across at him. "So what are you working on now?"

He grinned. "Stuff," he offered. "I really can't discuss ongoing cases."

"Can't blame a girl for trying. As long as you're trying to make a difference," she said.

The statement sat in the center of his chest like a fist. Right now, he was doing just the opposite of the main reason why he joined. As an agent, you were supposed to be objective and not let your personal feelings and prejudices interfere with your performance or your judgment. He knew both were compromised. He didn't believe in what he was doing to Ron Powers which contradicted everything he'd sworn to uphold.

The intermission ended and the comedy resumed. Dawne reached across the table and took his hand as she laughed at the comic on stage and Brian's conscience gave him another kick in the ribs.

"Thanks for a really great night. I can't remember the last time I had so much fun," Dawne said as they sat in Brian's car in front of her apartment building.

"Me, too. I really don't get out much."

"Then, maybe we can do it again sometime."

"I'd like that."

That awkward last moment of indecision hovered between them. Dawne, not one to wait for opportunity to present itself, made her own opportunity and leaned over and kissed him.

His lips were so soft, were her first thoughts, just as she imagined and when he put his arm around her and drew her close, she'd never felt that something could be more right.

His kiss was gentle and tender, so opposite of his very rigid persona. With his close-cut hair and clean-shaven face, no distinguishing marks, he could easily blend into a crowd, which worked well for the kind of work he did. But beneath that very controlled exterior, was a sensuality that burned just beneath the surface. That's the Brian that Dawne wanted to get to know.

Slowly, she eased back and watched his brown eyes slowly open. She smiled. "That was nice."

He almost looked shy for a moment, and that endeared him to her all the more.

"We'll have to try that again, too."

She sighed. "I better get inside." But she didn't move.

"I'll call you."

She opened the car door to the cool evening air. "Good night," she said before getting out, then closed the door behind her. She trotted up to the front steps of her building, turned and waved, then pushed through the heavy glass-and-chrome door.

For several moments, Brian sat in his car. Dawne was a great girl. He knew, just from the times they'd talked at the restaurant, that he wanted to get to know her better. After tonight, he was positive that this was a relationship that he wanted to pursue. But at what cost?

Dawne got out of her clothes and put on her oversized nightshirt. She crawled under the covers and turned out the light. She smiled contentedly, very pleased with herself. Whether Brian Jennings realized it or not, she was going after him full-steam ahead.

Her phone rang. She couldn't imagine who it could be at this hour. She peered at the caller ID and grinned.

"Yes, Desi…"

"Are you alone?"

"Yes! Do you think I'd bring a man home on the first date?"

"No telling with you. So how was it?"

Dawne purred. "Really nice. I'm mean, really

nice. He's attentive, funny, smart, good to look at. And the man can kiss."

"And he's gainfully employed," Desi added.

They laughed.

"I'm glad it worked out."

"Me, too."

"So I take it, you're going to see him again."

"That's the plan. He's going to call me."

"You sound really happy, sis."

"You know, I am." She giggled. "Anyway, I need to get some sleep and so do you."

"See you tomorrow."

"'Night."

Dawne hung up and rested her hands atop the covers. She was happy and she hoped it only got better.

Adam Collins sat outside Dawne's apartment building and watched Brian drive off. What the hell was going on?

Chapter 19

"Dawne and I had an ugly falling out the other day," Elizabeth was saying to Ron.

He was working on a wooden rack for her massive collection of jazz LPs, some real treasures.

"What happened?"

She told him about the conversation and how Dawne had flipped on her. Basically accusing her of abandoning her father in favor of him.

He put his tools down and looked at her over his shoulder. "You're kidding?"

She shook her head. "I wish I was." She got

up from being curled in the lounge chair and came to sit next to him on the floor. "Something else I need to tell you."

"Do I need a beer first?"

She chucked him in the arm. "I spoke with Matt."

His expression grew serious. "And?"

"He told me the real reason for his affair."

"His *real* reason?" he asked incredulously. He was already getting himself agitated. Every time he thought about what Matthew had put Ellie through, he wanted to push his fist through a wall.

Elizabeth put her hand on his shoulder. She could see him puffing up with every breath. "He, apparently, knew something was wrong with him long before the divorce…."

As Ron listened to her explain Matthew's rationale, he could almost sympathize with the man. For the most part, men valued themselves on several criteria, being able to provide for their families and being able to satisfy a woman. When one of those variables went out of sync they tended to lose not only their way but their sense of self. But the bigger question was, why was Elizabeth telling him all of this?

"Now that you know the truth, do you feel

that the divorce was a mistake?" he asked once she was done.

She lowered her gaze and tugged on her bottom lip with her teeth.

"Ellie? Was it a mistake? Are you planning to go back to him?"

Her eyes flew to his face and saw the subtle fear in the tightening of his brows.

"It's not as simple as that."

Ron put down his chisel, brushed his hands on his jeans and stood. He looked down at her. "Whatever you have to say, spit it out. I'm a big boy."

"What I'm trying to say is that of course the divorce was a mistake. It was a mistake because it was carried out under false pretenses."

Ron's insides took a nosedive. He didn't want to hear anymore.

"I went through with it because Matthew cheated on me with another woman and I firmly believed that he didn't love me anymore."

"Fine, Ellie. I get it okay. You now realize your ex-husband still loves you and that your divorce was a mistake. He's sick and needs you. I get it."

"Yep. Exactly." She stood up and grabbed him by the arm turning him to face her. She stared into his eyes. "And I'm in love with you. What Matthew did to me can't be undone. I'll admit, there was a moment when I thought that maybe we could make it work." She frowned and shook her head. "I won't go backward. Not at this stage of my life."

"But are you still in love with him, Ell? You need to be sure, and I damn sure do, too."

"I will always love Matthew, at least, the man that I married. But, no, I'm not in love with him. I'll help him through this crisis when I can. But I'm not going to allow him to play the guilt card with me. And I'm not going to allow him to interfere with us." Her voice softened. "Because *us* is too important to *me.*"

The hard lines of his face eased. He blew out a long breath. "Why you have to beat around the bush like that to tell a brotha you love him?" He fought to keep a straight face.

"Anything worth having is worth waiting for," she whispered.

He angled his head slightly to the side and put his arms around her waist. "I've been waiting for you for a long time, baby, and I'm thinking we need to make this more official than me just asking and you saying yes."

She frowned in confusion. "What do you mean?"

"I want to put something big, brilliant and expensive on that finger of yours."

Her heart fluttered in her chest. She grinned up at him, her eyes sparkling. "How big?"

He took her hand and pressed it to his chest. "As big as all that's in this old heart for you."

Her eyes suddenly filled. "I love you, Ronald Powers," she choked out.

"I think I'm starting to believe you." He lowered his head and took her mouth in a hungry, urgent kiss that stunned them with the unexpected intensity.

"We can't keep this up," she said breathlessly against his mouth.

"Who says so?" He lifted her up into his arms and carried her into her bedroom.

By the time they'd finally satisfied every need they had, at least for the day, they untangled themselves and took separate showers.

"No way am I getting into another shower with you," Elizabeth called out from the bedroom. "We'll never get out of here."

"Chicken."

"Name calling wins you no points."

"Did I tell you I saw that Jennings guy yesterday?"

She pushed open the bathroom door. Ron was standing in the center of the room, lean, muscular and very naked. She drew in a breath, momentarily forgetting her vow. She forced her eyes upward. "What did you say?"

"He came into the restaurant yesterday—to pick Dawne up for their date. Me and Ali were there."

"Oh, no. Why didn't you tell me?"

"Kinda pushed it out of my head. Guess I want the whole thing to just disappear." He leaned over the tub and turned on the shower, giving her a great view from the back. "It was real odd. He acted like he'd just met us for the first time so I let it ride. Ali almost had a heart attack, cause he had no clue about Dawne and this guy."

Elizabeth pushed out a frustrated breath. "This is all so crazy. What do they have on you? I simply don't understand and now with Dawne involved with this guy…is it part of some agenda of his?"

"I wish I knew. Maybe we ought to tell Dawne exactly what's happening. My thought is if he won't then maybe he is up to something."

She leaned against the frame of the door,

tossing around the information. "Maybe you're right." She looked at him. "Sooner rather than later?"

He nodded in agreement.

"Hey, Brian," Adam called out as he walked down the corridor.

Brian stopped and turned slightly. "I'm in a hurry, Adam."

Adam quickened his step and caught up with the taller man, matching him stride for stride. "We need to talk, partner."

"Really?" He flipped open a gray folder and scanned it as he continued walking. "About what?"

"About your relationship with Dawne Lewis."

Brian stopped short, snapped his head in Adam's direction. His eyes cinched. "You following me, man?"

"You trying to compromise this case?"

Brian got in Adam's face. "Look, what I do in my spare time is my business."

Adam flinched. "Not when it effects me. *Partner,*" he added. "You want to tell me what's going on or should I draw my own conclusions?" He raised a brow.

"Look, let me handle this. The minute I feel my actions will interfere with this case, I'll back off."

Adam looked at him for a long moment then turned and strode away.

Brian stood there for a moment. He had no idea what Adam planned to do with the information, but he couldn't let him ruin his career or his budding relationship with Dawne. He walked off to his office.

Chapter 20

"Let me find a parking space and I'll be right in," Ron said to Elizabeth.

"Okay." She got out of the car, opened her umbrella and made a dash into *Delectables*.

For a change, the restaurant was relatively quiet. Perhaps it was the weather. It had grown more and more dreary until the skies had opened up.

She shook off her umbrella and looked around for her daughters. Neither one of them were up front. She walked over to the counter.

"Hi, Ms. Lewis," the waitress greeted. "What

can I get for you or would you like to see a menu?"

"Actually, I was looking for my daughter, Dawne."

"I believe she's in the office putting in an order."

"Thanks." She spun around on the stool just as Ron walked in. He joined her, water dripping off him. He wiped his face with his hands.

"She's in the back," Elizabeth said.

"You sure you want to do this here," he asked having second thoughts.

"I don't think we should wait. It's not going to get easier."

"Okay." He followed her to the back where the tiny office was.

The door was closed and Elizabeth could hear Dawne talking. She knocked lightly on the door.

"Come in," she called out. Her face brightened in surprise then drew tight upon seeing the serious expressions on their faces. "Yes, that's it," she said into the phone, keeping her eye on her mother and Ron. "I can expect the delivery before noon tomorrow? Great. Thanks." She hung up the phone.

"What's going on?" Her hand still gripped the phone.

"We wanted to talk to you."

Dawne held up her hand. "First, before you say anything, I want to apologize about the other day. I was wrong and totally out of line."

"It's okay, honey, really."

"No. I was wrong. I had no right to assume things or speak to you like that." She took a breath. "I went to see Dad. We had a good talk… about everything." She gave her mother a meaningful glance. "He decided on his treatment. Desi went with him to his doctor's visit this morning."

Elizabeth briefly shut her eyes in thanks. Ron squeezed her hand.

"Thanks for telling me. But, more importantly, thanks for going to see your dad. I know it meant a lot to him."

"Is that why you came?"

Elizabeth shot a look at Ron.

"Actually, no," he said. "Mind if I sit down?"

Dawne gave a short nod.

Ron sat and Elizabeth sat next to him. She took his hand. "There's something that you need to know…about Brian."

Alternately, Ron and Elizabeth told Dawne everything they knew about the investigation into his business, his life and activities and their belief that he was somehow tied to illegal dealings with his supplier who was also under suspicion.

Dawne listened with her mouth partially opened. When they were done, she shook her head. "I don't believe this." She pushed up from the chair. "He's using me?"

"We don't know that for sure, Dawne," her mother said. "When he talked to me that day at the spa he sounded sincere. But he also made it clear that to stop seeing you was not in his plans and that, as long as he was dealing with the investigation, he was essentially the only friend we had."

Dawne's pinched expression looked almost painful. "He was threatening you," she said, appalled. She began pacing the tight space. "I... He used me to get to you, to find information about you?" She zeroed in on Ron. "And he walked right in here yesterday saw, you and acted like...nothing. God. How stupid could I be?"

"Dawne this has nothing to do with you being stupid. If, and I say if, this was his plan to get to us through you, there is no way you would have known," Ron assured her.

"He'd been coming here for weeks. He acted so interested," she said in a faraway voice remembering the kiss they'd shared the night before.

"Baby, he didn't want me to say anything, but

we—" she looked to Ron "—felt it best that you knew what you were dealing with."

Slowly, Dawne sat down, deflated. "I'll break it off. I have to," she said sounding beaten. "He's supposed to call me. I'll…talk to him then." She got up. "I have to get back to work."

"Sweetie," Elizabeth said, grabbing Dawne's hand as she passed, "it's going to be okay."

Dawne flashed a tight smile and walked out.

"Do you think we did the right thing?" Elizabeth asked. "Maybe we should have left it alone."

"No. If he's on the up and up regarding Dawne then it will come out. If he's not, that will come out, too. At least, she's not operating in the dark."

They both got up.

"Have you been able to reach your supplier?"

"No. I keep getting voice mail. I've left several messages, but there's been no response."

"Do they honestly believe that your wood supplier is somehow funding extremists?"

Ron opened the door for Elizabeth. "Apparently, they think he has some Middle East connection and the business is just a front to launder money."

"Even if that was the case," she said, walking out, "I still don't see how you are involved."

"Just the fact that I was once a part of a nationalist organization will make me a suspect until the end of time, no matter what my agenda may have been. The Panthers were targeted. Back then they were considered extremists and a threat to the country—or, at least, the status quo of the country."

"It's like a nightmare. Every day when I walk into the spa, I expect a dozen men in dark suits to come in and take over." She shuddered at the thought.

Ron put his arm around her. "This has got to be over soon."

She rested her head against his shoulder. "I hope so."

When they got up front, Dawne was behind the counter serving a customer. Her smile was in place but her eyes were distant. Her mother knew that look. It was Dawne preparing for action. She'd had that look in her eyes since she was a baby. If she saw something she wanted, she'd get that hunter's look in her eyes—even something as simple as zeroing in on a toy of her sister's. She didn't want to think about what Dawne was zeroing in on now.

Chapter 21

The rain was still coming down in buckets as Barbara made a break from her car to her front door. By the time she got inside, she was dripping wet.

Trudging up the stairs, she shook off water, leaving a wet trail. It had been a long day. To say that she was exhausted would be an understatement. She hung up her wet coat on the hook by the door and took her umbrella to the bathroom and put it in the tub.

She'd had a full day at the hospital and then had gone to the spa to work on three clients. Even though they had two wonderful massage staff, which they'd hired from the Swedish Institute, there were still her regular customers from the early days of the spa's opening that only wanted her.

She had to admit, that made her feel good— being wanted. She sighed. Wil wanted her to take the weekend off and take the trip with him down to North Carolina to see the house. On the surface, it was an innocent enough trip but, in her mind, it would signal some kind of unspoken agreement that she was willing to relocate. She knew he would ask her opinion, show her around, try to convince her how wonderful life could be for them. Maybe it would. What was she so afraid of?

Change wasn't easy, especially at her age. She wasn't some young thing that could just pick up and run behind a man. What if it didn't work out? She wouldn't have a job, a home. She had roots here in New York. Veronica'd said she was afraid of failing. Maybe she was. She didn't have the kind of time in her life to make mistakes and go back and fix them.

She got out of her clothes, put some leftovers in the oven to warm up, then went in the living room to watch some mindless television.

Surfing through the channels, she stopped when she saw Michael's face pop up on the screen. He was being interviewed by one of the hosts from *E!* Her heart fluttered for a moment. Sometimes it was still hard to believe that she'd almost married him. He was talking about being traded to New York. She turned up the volume.

"I'm excited about the trade," he was saying as he walked the red carpet on his way to an awards show. "There's no town like New York and I'm eager to be part of the historic team."

"But New York has had a lot of trouble with its players, management and, quite frankly, winning a championship."

"My job is to bring my A-game and to turn things around."

"We'll be looking forward to seeing you at Madison Square Garden, next week."

Her stomach rushed to the center of her chest. Next week? Michael was coming to New York? She got up from the couch and returned to the kitchen for her dinner.

Michael. He'd started off as a client at the hospital, then her lover, then her fiancé. Michael had reawakened her womanhood if he did nothing else. But when Wil stepped back into her life, whatever doubts she'd had about the big age gap between her and Michael only magnified.

Wil had provided her an out, gave voice to her

insecurities about being involved with a man young enough to be her son.

Barbara brought her dinner to the kitchen table and sat down heavily. Fears and doubts had affected her future with Michael. Now fears and doubts were affecting her future relationship with Wil.

She picked at her food and thought about her girlfriends. They were all secure with their men, making plans for their futures together. Why was it so hard for her?

The downstairs doorbell rang. She frowned. Probably someone needing to get into someone else's apartment. She ignored it. The bell rang again.

Making a face she pushed up from her seat and went to the intercom near the door.

"Who?"

"It's Chauncey, Ms. Barbara."

Chauncey? She pressed the button for the door and buzzed him in. Moments later. he was knocking on her front door.

"Chauncey, what are you doing here? Is something wrong?" She stepped aside to let him in. He pulled his hood off his head.

"Sorry to come by without calling, but I was on my way home from practice…"

"Come in. You can hang your jacket up right there." She pointed to the rack next to the door.

He took off his jacket and set his duffel bag down.

"I wanted to talk to you about something without Dad being around."

She was getting nervous.

"Okay." She walked into the living room and sat down.

Chauncey came in behind her and sat down. He fidgeted for a few minutes, looking at his laces. "Wow, this is harder than I thought."

"What is?"

"Saying what I got to say."

"Just talk," she said gently.

He blew out a breath. "In a few months I'll be going away to school, right?"

She nodded.

"And it'll be the first time me and Dad have been apart. I mean, since Mom died, it's just been me and him, ya know?" He looked around the room trying to find a place for his gaze to land. It eventually landed on the floor between his feet. "He's never been alone. Anyway... He's been working on getting this house for a long time. It's a dream of his and it's finally coming true. He told me that he wanted you to come with him and he asked me how I felt about that."

He finally looked at her. "At first, I didn't like it. I mean, it's one thing for Dad to have a girl… I mean, a woman in his life." He flashed an awkward smile. "But to live with someone…" He shrugged his right shoulder. "Anyway, I've been thinking about it a lot lately. I want him to be happy and I don't want him to be alone." He looked into her eyes. "He likes you a lot."

Her insides warmed.

"And, well, I was thinking that it would be a really good thing if you did go with him. I mean, I wouldn't mind or anything."

"I see."

"It would make him real happy. I know it would. My dad, he's a good guy, man— I mean, Ms. Barbara. He works hard and he's had no one for a long time—except for me. And now I'll be gone, ya know?" He suddenly stood up. "That's what I wanted to say. So, if you decided to go—" he shuffled his feet "—it would be cool."

Barbara didn't know what to say.

"I better get home. Dad will worry or start blowing up my cell phone." He grinned and looked just like his dad did at his age.

"Thank you for telling me that, Chauncey. It means a lot."

"Cool." He turned and headed to the door then stopped. "Don't tell Dad I was here. I don't want him to think I was all up in his personal business. Then he might think he can get in mine." He laughed.

"I won't say a word."

He bobbed his head, collected his things and walked out.

Barbara slowly closed the door behind him. Well, she'd gotten his son's blessing. So what was stopping her now?

Chapter 22

Ever since her mother and Ron had left the restaurant, Dawne's spirit was restless. Her emotions shifted from hurt to anger. If there was one thing that she detested it was people who used others for their own benefit.

She'd been advised not to say anything and just let it all play out. Although she'd agreed, she knew she couldn't let it rest and simply play along. It wasn't in her nature.

She stared at the phone—debating. Finally, she picked it up and dialed Brian's cell phone.

He picked up just before it went to voice mail.

After Dark

"Hey, Brian, it's Dawne."

"Hi. I was going to call you."

She rolled her eyes. "Beat you to it," she said, forcing lightness into her voice. "Listen, I'm not doing anything special this evening and I was wondering if you wanted to stop by. I'm fixing dinner now and you have to eat sometime."

"Uh, tonight?"

"Hey, if you have other—"

"No, no, tonight is fine. It's just that I'm in my car right now. What time were you thinking about?"

"Around eight?"

"Sounds good. I'll see you in a little while."

"Great. See you soon." She hung up the phone, her expression set in determination. Nobody was going to play her.

Brian checked his rearview mirror. Ever since his little run in with Adam earlier in the day, he'd been looking over his shoulder. He knew Adam would do just about anything to get ahead in the department even if it meant fabricating information and turning on his partner. He couldn't let that happen. First thing in the morning, he was going to Hargrove to tell him everything he knew, but first, he needed to set things straight with Dawne. He made the turn and headed uptown.

Traffic was light considering the hour and the crappy weather. He arrived in front of Dawne's building with nearly a half hour to spare. He found a parking space after several tries, looked around for Adam's car, then walked half a block to Dawne's building.

"I don't usually get dinner invitations in the middle of the week," he said when she opened the door for him.

"I'm glad you accepted," she said, taking his umbrella to the bathroom. "Make yourself comfortable," she called out.

"Something sure smells good," he said.

Dawne returned to the small living room that also served as the dining room. "Nothing special, but I hope you'll like it. So…how was your day?"

"The usual."

"Hmm, top secret, huh?" She forced herself to smile.

"Not really, just the usual." He sat on the small couch.

Dawne sat opposite him on the matching arm chair.

Brian looked around. "You have a really nice place."

"Thanks. It's small, but it works. Can I get you something to drink?"

He nodded. "Sure."

She got up and headed for the kitchen. "Juice, water, iced tea?"

"Juice is fine."

She was steaming and it took all she had not to launch right into him. But she planned to bide her time. She opened the fridge and took out the container of juice. She jumped when she'd turned and saw Brian standing in the doorway watching her.

"Sorry, I didn't mean to startle you."

"Hope you don't always creep around like that," she said, sputtering a nervous laugh.

"I need to talk to you," he blurted out.

She looked at him. "Okay." She took a glass from the cabinet, poured his juice and handed it to him. "I'm listening," she said. She folded her arms.

"This isn't easy and I don't know where to begin." He drew himself up and focused on her. "I like you, Dawne, a lot."

"Is that a bad thing?"

"Yeah, sort of."

"Oh. I see."

"Whatever you're thinking, it's not like that."

You have no idea what I'm thinking.

He looked uncomfortable, shifting from one foot to the other. "I'm working on a case that involves your mother's friend, Ron."

She could not have been more stunned by his revelation, but she played along. "I beg your pardon."

"Part of my job is to compile a list of potential threats to security."

"How in the world could Ron be a threat to security?"

"I don't know how much you know about his past…"

She didn't respond.

"When he was a teenager, he was a member of the Black Panther Party. Well, the government always keeps track of anyone who's ever been in any kind of militant group, no matter how big or small. They build a file that basically never goes away." He shoved his hands into his pants pockets. "Anyway, the FBI has been working with Homeland Security to check out everyone who's ever appeared on the list, bring their files up to date and cross-check the names with any affiliations that appear suspect.

"Ron's name came up and his association with

a supplier in Philadelphia who we believe is getting money from the Middle East."

"And *you* think Ron is involved in some kind of way? Is that what you're saying?"

"Just the opposite. I know he's not. What I've been trying to do is prove that. My partner on the other hand—"

"The guy that comes with you to the restaurant?"

"Yeah. He feels differently." He hesitated. "See, the thing is, until I can prove otherwise, Adam is determined to take Ron down...and your mother, if necessary."

Dawne slowly sat down.

"The thing is, Adam found out that I was seeing you outside of the restaurant."

"How?"

"He...followed me the night we went out."

"What?"

"I'm in a real bad situation. I've compromised the investigation by being involved with you because of your relationship with Ron through your mother."

She pressed her hands to her head. "This is crazy."

"The crazy thing is, I need to break this off between us or I could lose my job."

Dawne raised her head and looked him in the eyes. What she saw there surprised her—regret.

"But I don't intend to. But, if I turn over the case to Adam in order to stay with you, he'll railroad Ron right to a grand jury."

Her heart thumped. "What are you saying?"

"I'm saying that I have to stay on the case to be sure that Ron gets a fair deal. And I'm saying that, if you can see your way clear, I want to keep seeing you."

"You're willing to risk your job for me?" she asked incredulously.

"I'm hoping it won't come to that."

"I—I don't know what to say."

"I hope you'll say you'll at least think about it. I know it's a lot to absorb, but—"

"I need to tell you something, the real reason why I asked you here," she said cutting him off.

Brian frowned. "The real reason?"

She ran her tongue across her lips. "My mother and Ron came to the restaurant…"

She told him about their conversation.

"I was so angry and hurt, I saw red," she confessed. "I thought you were somehow using me to get to them or, if you hadn't, already, you would. They told me not to say anything to let it play out, but—not me."

"I couldn't do that to you," he said gently. "I'm glad you called." He paused. "I have another confession to make."

"Do I want to hear it?" she said with a half smile.

"I liked you from when we were in college, but you wouldn't give me the time of day. When I ran into you at the restaurant I figured fate had stepped in to give me another chance."

She looked at him in amazement. "Why didn't you ever say anything?"

He shrugged. "I was shy, kinda awkward and you were always surrounded by your friends."

"Wow," was all she could say. "I always thought you were kinda cute." She grinned. "But you kinda kept to yourself."

"Everything happens in its own time, as my grandmother always said."

"We're here now," she said softly.

"Yeah, we are, aren't we?" He slowly approached her.

She looked up at him and again saw the warmth and sincerity in his eyes; the doorways to the soul.

"I don't know how all of this is going to pan out," he said, gazing down at her, "but I'm going to do my damnedest to make it work out for everyone."

"But your job…"

"I'll be up front with you. This whole thing,

investigating our own people, leaves a real sour taste in my mouth. I didn't like the assignment from the beginning and maybe I didn't put my all into it because of that. But I have reason now." His eyes slowly traversed her face. "And, most of all, I want to give us a shot. A real one."

She took his hand. "You really are special."

"Think so?"

"Yeah, I do."

"So now what?"

"Let's start fresh," she said. "I like you a lot, Brian. Maybe more now because you've been so honest with me about everything. I want to see where this is going to go, too."

"That's what I wanted to hear."

After Brian left for the evening, Dawne had time to put things in perspective. She'd been so gung ho to point the finger of accusation without giving Brian a chance. It was a quirk in her personality that had gotten her into plenty of scrapes—leaping before she looked.

This time she liked what she saw. Maybe it would work out and maybe it wouldn't, but she would give it a chance.

In the meantime, she hoped that Brian's gut instincts about Ron were true.

Chapter 23

"You have a call on line two," Sterling's secretary said.

"Thanks." He depressed the flashing red light.

"Yes, Sterling Chambers."

"This is Agent Jennings.

Sterling sat up in his chair. "Yes, Agent Jennings?"

"I understand that you're the attorney for both Ron Powers and the owners of the spa. I was hoping that we could meet. I'm in your area. I could be there in five minutes."

"Sure."

"Good, I'll see you shortly."

He buzzed his secretary. "Stacy, I'm expecting a visitor in a few minutes, a Mr. Jennings. When he arrives, show him right in and hold all my calls."

"Of course, Mr. Chambers."

He disconnected the intercom and leaned back in his seat. What did Jennings want? He had a feeling it wasn't good news, but he hoped he was wrong.

As promised, Brian was walking through the doors of Sterling's office five minutes later. He must have been right outside, Sterling thought.

"Agent Jennings—" he extended his hand to the young man "—I'm sure this isn't a social call so let's get to it. Have a seat." He pointed toward the leather seat opposite his desk.

Brian sat down and unbuttoned his jacket. "Thank you."

Sterling waited for him to explain his sudden appearance.

"I had a meeting with my supervisor this morning regarding this case. He's really pushing."

"And you're telling me this…because?"

"Everything that I've turned up on Powers is a dead end. Everything that involves his wood supplier in Philly is a dead end. Turns out, the reason why no one could get in touch with him and his business is temporarily closed is because he had a heart attack. He's been in the hospital for the past two weeks."

Sterling shook his head. "So he wasn't trying to avoid anyone."

"Not at all. The agent down in Philly just got back to me with the information this morning."

"Unbelievable. You guys aren't very efficient. So, I guess it's all over."

"No. That's why I'm here. I have a search warrant for Powers's business and for the accounting records at the spa." He handed Sterling the warrant.

"Let me see that." He snatched it from Brian's hands. He snapped the papers open and read the request. He looked at Brian. "I'm going with you."

"I was hoping you'd say that."

Sterling got up and put on his jacket. "Let's go." He stopped at his secretary's desk. "I'll be out for the rest of the afternoon. Call Judge Melvin's chambers and get a postponement for the hearing this afternoon."

"Yes, Mr. Chambers."

Sterling stormed out. He got to the elevator and whirled on Brian, shaking the warrant in his face. "This is a crock, and you know it."

"I'm doing my job."

Sterling glared at him. "How do you sleep at night, railroading innocent people?"

Brian looked away. It was going to get ugly, but it was the only way he could ensure that he was the one handling the ugliness and not Adam.

When Sterling got downstairs, he saw a cop car parked out front.

"Brought your boys, I see," Sterling said.

"I didn't have to come to you. It was a courtesy. We could have gone straight to the locations and let your clients call you."

Sterling knew he was right, but he was still pissed. He didn't reply.

"We're going to Powers's place, first," Brian told the driver of the police car. "You can ride with me," he said to Sterling.

When they arrived at Ron's office, Sterling walked in first. Ron looked up from the desk and knew it had to be bad news.

"I had a visit from the FBI." He showed Ron the warrant. "Give them whatever they need and don't say a word. It's only a warrant for your accounting records."

Ron gritted his teeth. "Fine."

The two officers walked in followed by Brian. Ron wanted to punch him right between the eyes. Instead, he led the two officers to the back room.

Sterling stood in stony silence while the officers did their work. Shortly, they came out with two huge boxes each and went to the patrol car out front.

"Now what?" Ron asked Sterling.

"They'll go through your records try to make some kind of connection…and, when they don't, they'll return everything."

"How long is this going to take?"

"Hopefully, not too long. In the meantime, don't make any transactions of any kind."

"What about paying my guys?"

"Pay them and that's it. Look, I gotta go. They want the spa's records, too."

Ron sputtered an expletive as Sterling walked out.

Carmen was at the front desk with they arrived at the spa. Sterling talked to Carmen who told him that Barbara and Elizabeth were downstairs.

Sterling went down first and headed for the office. The door was partially open. Elizabeth was inside. He was surprised to see Ann Marie. He'd thought she was showing Stephanie and Tony some more houses today.

"Sterling…what…" Ann Marie saw the uniforms behind him and the smile vanished from her mouth.

Elizabeth immediately recognized Brian.

Their eyes flew to Sterling.

"They have a warrant to seize all of your accounting records."

"What?" Elizabeth felt weak.

"Is Barbara here?"

"She's with a client."

"Maybe you should go and get her," Sterling advised.

Elizabeth couldn't move.

Ann Marie snapped out of her shock and went to get Barbara.

Sterling explained what was going on.

"This is a travesty," she said.

"Give them what they need, Barbara," Sterling quietly advised.

She glared at the officers and Brian, in particular. "Fine. They're in that filing cabinet," she finally said, and pointed to an old metal cabinet in the corner.

Elizabeth came up to Sterling. "What about Ron?"

"They've been there, already."

She briefly shut her eyes. "This is a nightmare."

Ann Marie planted her hand on her hip and zeroed in on Brian. "You should be ashamed of yourself! What kinda man you be turnin' on your own people?"

Sterling grabbed her arm. "Ann. Be quiet. He's doing his job."

She let out a string of Jamaican curses that no one could understand, and snatched away from Sterling.

The officers collected what they'd come for and left without a word.

"Now what?" Barbara asked. She was shaking all over.

"Like I explained to Ron, they'll go over everything and, when then turn up nothing, they'll return your property."

"Is Ron okay?" Elizabeth asked.

"Under the circumstances, yes, he's fine."

"I'm sorry about this," Brian said.

All eyes turned on him.

"I'm sorry," he repeated, and walked out.

"What do we do now?" Barbara asked Sterling.

"Go on with your business as usual. Hopefully this whole thing won't take long. I have to get back to my office. I'll call you later," he said to Ann Marie. He kissed her lightly on the lips and walked out.

The trio stood in silence, each caught up in their own turbulent thoughts.

* * *

A team of examiners were set up to go over the material once Brian returned to the office.

"Do a thorough job and do it quickly," he instructed. He left them in the work room and went to call Dawne. He hoped to get to her before anyone else did.

Chapter 24

The ladies were gathered at Barbara's house. The mood was dismal.

"This is so ugly," Ann Marie said.

"There's something I need to tell you all," Elizabeth said.

All eyes turned on her.

"Dawne has been seeing Agent Jennings."

"What?" they shouted.

Elizabeth went on to explain.

"What a creep," Terri said.

"That's putting it mildly," Stephanie added.

"Now that she knows, I'm sure she'll find a

way to break it off with him without letting him know that she is aware of what's going on," Elizabeth assured them.

"Just playing devil's advocate 'ere, but what if they do find whatever it is they're looking for in Ron's records." She looked at Elizabeth who had a mortified expression on her face.

"Ann!" Barbara snapped.

"How could you say something like that?" Elizabeth asked.

"You always put your foot in your mouth," Stephanie said.

"I'm just asking a question. Now *I'm* the bad guy." She popped up from her seat and marched over to the table to fix a drink.

"I hate to say this," Terri spoke up, "but having spent years in advertising and marketing, it's no different from the government. They can make something out of nothing if they try hard enough."

Stephanie concurred. "We need to be able to put a plan in place in the event that…they do find something."

Elizabeth was livid. "Since when did we start assuming that someone was guilty until proven innocent!"

"Ell, that's not—"

"I don't want to hear your rational take on it, Barbara, so save it."

Her vehemence rocked Barbara back on her heels.

"Ellie, we're all friends here," Stephanie said.

"Are we? Friends don't say things like that to friends."

"Ellie you are blowing this way out of proportion," Barbara said.

Elizabeth's eyes filled with tears. "I'm leaving. You all stay and figure out a plan—when they find Ron guilty of something." She grabbed her purse and ran out.

"Maybe you should go after her, Barbara," Terri said.

Barbara slowly sat down. In all the years she'd known Elizabeth, she'd never seen her like that. "I think Ellie may need some time to herself."

"When she calms down, she'll see we didn't mean any harm. But, the reality is, we do have a business to consider," Stephanie said.

Murmurs of agreement went all around.

"Terri and I will work out a statement, just in case, and we'll certainly have to reassure our clients if this turns the wrong way."

Barbara sighed heavily. When they'd all sat together months ago and came up with the plan for the spa, never in their wildest dreams, would they have imagined the series of recent events. And she certainly would never have imagined Ellie turning on her. That stunned and hurt her most of all.

"I'm kind of beat," Stephanie said with a yawn. "This pregnancy knocks the stuffing out of me. Can't hang like I used to."

"I better go, too," Terri said. "Michael is coming over later."

"When are we going to get to meet him?" Ann Marie asked.

"Soon. We'll all have to get together once the dust settles."

"Barbara, are you going to be okay?" Stephanie asked. They all knew how close she and Elizabeth were and how hard it must be for her to have listened to Elizabeth go off on her like that.

With sad eyes, Barbara looked up at her departing guests. "Sure, I'll be fine. I think I'll turn in early anyway."

They said their goodbyes and filed out, one by one.

For a long while, Barbara sat alone in her living room, Elizabeth's lashing out at her still fresh in her mind. Even in the midst of all that was going on, Elizabeth didn't waver in her belief in Ron, so much so that she was willing to turn on her friends. She loved him, really loved him.

She got up and went into her bedroom. She sat on the side of the bed and picked up the phone.

Chapter 25

Elizabeth put her key in her door and wearily walked inside. She didn't know if she was happy or disappointed to see Ron sitting in her living room.

"Hi," he said.

"I wasn't expecting you." She deposited her purse on the table in the hall and dropped her keys inside.

"I hope you don't mind," he said, suddenly feeling uncomfortable.

"No." She didn't look at him. "Did you eat?" She walked into the kitchen.

Ron followed her to the kitchen and came up behind her. He put his arms around her waist and pressed his head against the back of hers. "I'm so sorry for all of this, baby."

Tears slowly trickled down her cheeks. "What are we going to do, Ron?"

"Everything is going to be fine, baby, I swear to you."

He turned her around to face him. She looked up into his eyes. "Do you believe that, believe in me?"

She nodded her head.

"That's all I need." He pulled her close.

Once upon a time her life had been so simple, she thought, listening to the beat of his heart. She'd been in a sensible marriage, had two beautiful children and wonderful friends. Then suddenly, she was thrust into a new life, a new relationship, only to discover that the life she'd left behind was all based on a lie and mistrust. Now, here she was, betting it all on a man who could very well not be what he seemed.

But deep in her heart, down in her soul, she believed in this man who held her as if his whole world depended on it. She inhaled deeply and drew in his comforting scent and a sense of peace slowly began to fill her.

She eased back and looked up at him. "I love you," she whispered, and knew she'd never felt more sure. "I promised myself that night I walked out of Matt's apartment, that I wasn't ever going to let doubt and mistrust enter my life again." She stroked his cheek. "Whatever happens, we're in this together."

"You won't regret it, Ell. I promise you that. And, when this is all over I'm going to prove it to you."

"How about starting now," she whispered against his mouth.

A half smiled curved his mouth. "Right now?"

"Right here."

"On the table?" he asked, his eyes darkening. His hands slid down to her hips.

"It's the only place we haven't tried."

"Ms. Lewis, you are getting very kinky."

"Right." She began unbuttoning his shirt. "So try to keep up." She stripped him of his shirt and tossed it on the floor.

He pushed her skirt up around her hips and lined her neck with steamy kisses.

Elizabeth backed up to the table that easily sat six. Effortlessly, she hopped up and pulled Ron behind her legs.

"I think I'm going to like this," he said on a hot breath.

"I know you will." She unfastened his pants and pushed them down, the urge to solidify their union erupting like a sudden fire in the forest. It started as a spark then grew and spread, getting hotter and more intense.

Ron didn't bother with her panties, he simply pushed them aside. Elizabeth raised her hips and spread her thighs wider. He grabbed her rear and pulled her toward him.

A searing heat shot up inside her. She gasped and held on.

Ron groaned deep in his throat in that first instant when he felt her wrap tightly around him. He took her slow and deep the way they both liked it. But this time was new, different somehow. This time, it was more than the thrill of being together and satisfying each other. This time, it was about sealing their bond, confirming their trust and the love they had for each other.

He swore, as the love he had for her poured out of him, that he would never let her regret the decision she'd made, no matter what it took.

"What are you going to do about the business until this mess is finished?" Elizabeth asked as they snuggled together in her bed.

"I have a job that I'm working on now. Ali and I decided that we are going to try to stall the next one for as long as we can. There's no telling what they may pull out of their sleeves and I don't want to get caught in the middle of a job and have to stop."

She nodded against his chest. "Makes sense."

"Have you talked to Dawne?"

"No. I probably should have called her but I didn't know what to say and I didn't want to get her any more involved."

"It's probably best."

She pressed closer to the warmth of his body. "I hope so."

"When all of this is settled, I want us to go away for a little while," Ron said. The ring he'd purchased for her two weeks earlier was burning a hole in his pocket. It had been on the tip of his tongue so many times to ask her to marry him, but the time was never quite right and then it was one crisis after another. And now seemed totally inappropriate.

"I'd like that," she said.

Maybe it could be more than a getaway—a honeymoon. He closed his eyes and silently prayed that the mess would be over quickly and quietly so that he and Ellie could get on with the life he wanted to give her.

* * *

"You did what?" Dawne screamed into the phone.

She listened in horror as Brian told her about the execution of the search warrants. "I don't believe this," she muttered, pacing the room, her thoughts racing. "You told me everything was going to be all right. I trusted you!"

"Dawne, listen to me. I didn't lie to you. If I didn't get the warrants it would give my boss plenty of reason to take me off the case and put Adam in charge. We knew the warrants were a possibility from the beginning."

As she listened she didn't know what to believe.

"There are a bunch of guys going over everything. I'm pretty sure we'll have what we need by the end of the week."

"And then what—a public hanging!" She was so angry the pulse in her temples pounded.

"I'm on top of it. You're going to have to trust me."

She flopped down in an empty seat in the kitchen. "I don't have to do jack. But one thing I will do, is make you wish you'd never met me if you're lying." She slammed down the phone. Had she just threatened an FBI agent? She was losing it.

Chapter 26

It had been a little more than a week since the records had been confiscated. Brian hadn't spoken to Dawne and he didn't expect to hear from her.

As bad as it was, he had to smile. If nothing else, Dawne Lewis had heart. She had no qualms about making it clear what she would do to him and didn't give a damn that he was the law.

"Guess you'll be happy."

Brian glanced up. Adam walked into his space. He had a folder in his hand. "I took the liberty of reviewing the report." He dropped it on

Brian's desk. "Hargrove wants to see you in his office." He walked out.

Brian drew the folder toward him. His case number was on the front cover. He flipped it open. Finally, a feeling a calm eased through him.

He took the folder and headed for Hargrove's office. He knocked.

"Come in."

"You wanted to see me?"

"Have a seat, Jennings."

He did as he was told.

"I was given a copy of the report on Powers and the contractor in Philadelphia."

"Yes, sir."

"Good job."

"Thank you, sir."

"But I have another issue, Jennings."

His muscles tensed.

"It was brought to my attention that you somehow got yourself involved with a woman who was indirectly associated with the case."

Adam.

"I didn't realize that at first, sir."

"Yes, but when you did, you pursued the relationship, anyway, didn't you?"

He chose not to respond to the rhetorical question.

"You do realize that, if we had to prosecute this case, you could have single-handedly ruined it?"

"Yes…sir."

Hargrove pursed his lips then steepled his fingers in front of him. "I was very concerned about your actions, but chose not to intervene, just to see what you would do. Adam's actions didn't surprise me, but yours did."

"Sir?"

"You followed through with this case to the letter. I would think that couldn't have been easy. Based on that, I'm going to let this one indiscretion of yours go away as if it never existed. And I'm reassigning you a new partner. If there's anyone I hate more than a brown nose, it's a snitch."

Brian sat in shock.

"That's all, Jennings."

He swallowed. "Thank you, sir." He rose.

"And, Jennings…"

"Yes, sir?"

"The next time you decide to get involved with someone, use those skills you have and check them out, first. I'd hate to have to revisit this issue with you."

"Yes, sir. Thank you."

He walked out feeling as if he'd been spared the firing squad. Hurrying back to his office, he didn't know who to call first.

Barbara looked up from the reception desk as two men in suits walked in carrying several file boxes. They approached the desk.

"We're looking for a Barbara Allen."

"I'm Barbara Allen."

They placed the boxes on the desk. "Sign here please." He passed her a form.

"What is it?" She looked at the miniscule type.

"A letter releasing your documents back to you along with a confidentiality statement."

She took her time and read every word. She didn't want her signature to come back and haunt her. Finally, she signed it and handed it back.

"Thank you, ma'am." Without another word they turned and walked out.

She opened the lid to the first box and saw that it contained the receipts as did the others. She breathed a sigh of relief then picked up the phone and called Sterling's office.

"Two men in suits were just here. They brought our records back."

"Yeah, I just got off the phone with Jennings.

He told me. I didn't get a chance to call you. Is everything there?"

"It looks like it. Does this mean that it's finally over?"

"Yes. Jennings said that the investigation turned up nothing on the spa, Ron or the supplier."

"Thank God," she said on a breath.

"I need to call Ron and make sure everything is good on his end."

"Sure. Go ahead and thanks for everything."

"I didn't do anything. The wheels of justice grind slowly but right won out. That's what important."

Barbara hung up the phone just as Stephanie came in.

"Are those what I think they are?" she asked pointing at the boxes.

Barbara nodded.

Stephanie placed her hand on her hip acting totally put out. "And to think that we spent hours crafting such an eloquent media release decrying the injustice of the federal government."

Barbara laughed. "Just be thankful you didn't have to use it."

"You got that right. Did you tell the others?"

"Not yet, they just left before you came up."

"Have you spoken to Ellie since the other night?" she inquired softly.

"No. Not really. She took the week off and she hasn't called me."

"She's just being stubborn. She'll come around."

"I know." She picked up one of the boxes. "Looks like we have cause to celebrate."

"Ain't gotta call me twice to a party." She reached for a box and tucked it under her arm.

They went downstairs together.

"Tony and I found the house we wanted," Stephanie said when they'd gotten down to the office.

"You're kidding? That's wonderful."

Stephanie grinned. "It's perfect. A two-family house in a nice neighborhood, near transportation, all new appliances, backyard."

"Stephanie, it sounds fabulous. Now we really do have to celebrate."

"There's enough room for my little family." She patted her stomach. "And Samantha."

"You're really going to bring Sam to live with you?"

"Yeah. I miss her. And she's doing well."

"That's wonderful." She gathered her in a hug. "You're taking on a lot, with a new baby, boyfriend and your sister, but, if anyone can handle it, you can."

"Thanks. But I have one correction." She stepped out of Barbara's arms.

Barbara frowned. "What?"

Stephanie stuck out her left hand and the diamond caught the light.

"Oh, my goodness," Barbara squealed, admiring the beautiful diamond ring. "Stephanie getting married. Lawd, lawd! Have you set a date?"

"We want to get married before the baby comes and before I blow up like a house and can't fit into anything absolutely exquisite." She giggled. "We're thinking in about a month."

"A month!" She pressed her hand to her chest. "That doesn't give us much time to plan. We have to have a shower, find your dress…" Her mind was off and running.

"I want you to be my maid of honor, Barbara."

She froze. "You do?"

"I wouldn't want anyone else, other than my sister. You've been my anchor since I met you and you always believed in me and gave me confidence when I didn't have any. You saw me through the mess with Conrad and didn't sling it in my face. You've been a friend, Barbara, a true dear friend and I hope you say yes."

Barbara's heart was so full she felt it well up in her eyes. "I would be honored," she was finally able to say.

Stephanie hugged her tightly. "Thank you."

Barbara blinked back tears. "Party, Friday night, my place."

"You're on."

When Barbara went home that night she worked on the menu for Stephanie's engagement, new-house-announcement party. She had some news to share with her friends, as well.

Chapter 27

Elizabeth was floating on air. Ron had called from his office to deliver the good news. The terrible ordeal was finally behind them and now they could all move on with their lives.

He said he would be coming over later to celebrate. As she prepared for his arrival she knew she had some things to take care of herself.

She'd been so awful to Barbara and she knew it the moment she'd stormed out on her. But she'd been so upset and hurt that she'd dug in her heels and wouldn't budge. Guess her feisty daughter, Dawne, got her headstrong ways honestly.

She finished seasoning the pot roast and put it in the Crock-Pot to cook. She owed Barbara an apology big-time and there was no time like the present. She checked the flame under the pot and went downstairs to the spa.

When she entered the spa and saw all the usual activity a sense of pride filled her. They had done this. Four friends with a dream and Barbara at the helm, the unwavering force that held them together.

She crossed the cool wood floor and went to the front desk.

"Hey, Carmen. Is Barbara around?"

"She's in the café with Ann Marie's daughter, Raquel."

"Thanks." She headed for the café and found Barbara and Raquel chatting in the back on the lounge chairs. With her tail between her legs she approached.

"Hello, ladies."

They both looked up.

"Hi, Ms. Ellie. I haven't seen you in a while." She got up and kissed Elizabeth's cheek.

"Good to see you."

"I came to meet Drew and was talking to Ms. Barbara about some ideas I've been toying with for alterations to the design of the reception area."

"Whatever they are, I know they'll be fabulous."

Raquel had been responsible for all of the interior work of the spa from picking out furniture, to its placement, to the artwork that hung on the walls.

Raquel checked her watch. "I better go. Drew's waiting for me up front."

"Take care, Raquel, and when you're ready with the designs, bring them by."

"I will." She waved and hurried off.

Elizabeth turned to Barbara. "Mind if I sit down?"

"Of course not."

Elizabeth took a seat. She folded her hands in her lap. "I don't know where to begin except to say how sorry I am. I've been a crazy fool these past weeks and I think I might have lost my mind along the way." She looked at her friend of two decades. "There's no way that you would intentionally hurt me, and I know that. You've always had my best interests at heart. And I can't tell you how sorry I am for dumping my anger and frustration out on you."

"Ellie, we're friends. I know you were hurting inside." She sighed. "But something you said, hit home."

Elizabeth flinched.

"Barbara, the rational one." She smiled sadly. "That's me. Always thinking things through until I wear a hole in it. Sometimes you have to go with your feelings. I've learned that lesson over and over these past few weeks, from every direction."

"Barbara, I didn't mean it like—"

"It doesn't matter, it's true and I accept that. It's who I am, who I've been." She took Elizabeth's hand. "Apology accepted. And to assure you of that, you have to come to the party at my house Friday night. We have so much to celebrate."

Elizabeth smiled with relief. "Absolutely!"

They talked for a few minutes more with Elizabeth bringing Barbara up to date on Matt's treatment and how the girls had stepped in to take some of the pressure off of her.

"You raised 'em good," Barbara said. "Matt is a lucky man."

"Hmm, that he is."

"Well, go on and finish your day off," Barbara said. "You'll be back at the grind looking at all of these hunks day after day before you know it."

Elizabeth giggled. "Girl, it's a hard job…"

"But somebody's got to do it," they said in unison.

"I have some celebrating of my own to do to-night with Ron. He's coming over after work." She gave Barbara a wink.

"Then get to it. I'll talk with you later."

Elizabeth got up. "Thanks," she said softly.

"For what?"

"For being Barbara." She turned and walked out.

By the time she got back upstairs to her apartment the space was filled with mouthwatering aroma. She finished up with the side dishes then went to look for something sexy to put on after a nice long, sudsy bath.

By the time she was done with all of her preparations, she heard Ron's key in the door. Just the simple sound of it made her tingle inside. Her man was home.

She barely let him in the door before she was in his arms. She linked her fingers behind his head and gazed up into his eyes.

"Welcome home," she said, before offering him a soft kiss of greeting.

"A man could get used to this real easy," he said, holding her close.

"I hope so." She took his hand and pulled him inside behind her. "Sit down and relax. Tonight is your night. Dinner is ready and will be served momentarily," she said in a sad British accent. She skipped off to the kitchen to prepare their plates.

When she returned to the living room, Ron had dimmed the lights and turned on the music in her CD player. Kem, her favorite singer was on.

"Hmm, nice," she murmured.

He got up to help her with the plates.

They sat side by side.

"Smells wonderful," he said, but didn't make an attempt to eat.

She looked at him quizzically. "Try some. Tell me how it tastes."

He shifted in his seat a few times. Looked at her, then looked away.

"Ell, I, uh, I've never done this before."

Her brow wrinkled in confusion. "Done what?"

He bit down on his lip. "I've wanted to, but…"

"Ron, you're making me nervous. What is it?"

He huffed, dug in his pants pocket and pulled out a black velvet box.

Her heart began hammering in her chest.

"I know I've asked…in a way. But I want to make it official." He opened the box and the most beautiful diamond set on a gold band gleamed at her. "Ellie, I love you with all my being. And I promise if you give me the chance I'll make you happy every day for the rest of our lives. Be my wife, Ell, my partner, my friend. Marry me. Please?"

"I'll have to cook pot roast more often," she blabbered, the tears rolling down her cheeks. "Yes, yes, yes, I'll marry you. I said it before but I'll say it again, Ronald Powers, I would love to be your wife."

Chapter 28

Brian wasn't sure what kind of reception he was going to get when he walked into *Delectables,* but, knowing Dawne's temper, he figured a public place was best.

He opened the doors and the chimes jingled. Desiree was behind the counter. Cautiously, he approached.

"We were just about to close for the night. I can get you something to take out," she said.

"Actually, I was hoping to find your sister."

"She left early. She took my father for his treatment today and then she said she was going home."

His hopeful expression sunk. "Oh. Thanks." He turned to leave.

Desiree came from around the counter. "Brian, wait."

He stopped and turned to face her.

"Look, I generally don't get in Dawne's business. But, this time, I think I should." She folded her arms. "She told me what's been going on—everything."

"I see."

"Look, Dawne can be hotheaded sometimes and run off at the mouth. And there's no telling what she might do if she gets really pissed off. But she really likes you. All of this mess just threw her for a loop for a minute."

"I like her, too."

"I think she would be very happy to see you if you happened to stop by her apartment."

"You sure?" he asked, sounding like a kid.

"Very. If I know anybody, I know my sister."

"Thanks." He grinned, and Desiree saw how cute he actually was in a straitlaced kind of way.

He turned to leave.

"Oh, don't tell her I sent you. I truly do not want to hear that girl's mouth."

Brian chuckled. "Your secret is safe with me."

All day long, he'd wanted to call her and tell her everything that had happened, but he needed to see her face to face and look in her eyes.

He pulled up in front of her building. It took him a few minutes to get his act together before he rang her bell.

"Who is it?" she asked through the intercom.

"It's Brian. Can I come up?"

"It's about time," she said. "I thought you'd never get here."

She pressed the buzzer, and Brian grinned all the way to the elevator and up to her front door.

When she opened the door and kissed him full on the lips, he knew that, whichever way things went with Dawne, it was going to be a wild ride.

Chapter 29

Friday Night

Each guest that arrived at Barbara's seemed to bring a new level of excitement. They were almost giddy with their laughter, talking all at once, hugging each other.

Everyone was gathered around the table filling their plates, when, suddenly, Ann Marie squealed and pointed at Stephanie.

"Is that what I think it is?" she asked.

Stephanie beamed. "Yep. A big old fat diamond ring. I'm going to get me a husband to go with this baby and my new house."

Everyone gathered around to "ooh" and "aah" over Stephanie's ring.

"Well, you need to go down the aisle first," said Ann Marie, "with that baby coming. And me gon come right behind you!" She stuck out her hand and flashed her newly acquired ring.

Another round of screams and yells and jumping up and down.

"Gosh, can't I do anything first around here," proclaimed Elizabeth.

They all turned to her and were greeted by a smile bright enough to light up Times Square. Demurely, she showed off her engagement ring. "Got it two days ago. Don't know how I was able not to tell the world."

"Oh, congratulations! I'm so happy for you," Stephanie said. "You and Ron are made for each other."

"Thank you, thank you. I'm deliriously happy."

Stephanie put her hand on her hip and scanned the group. "Okay, anybody else?"

Terri's brows shot up. "Hey, I got mine for New Year's, but I'll be happy to show it off again." She did a slow pirouette with her hand stretched out in front of her.

They all cracked up laughing.

Barbara stood slightly to the side relishing in the joy of her friends. "Ladies," she said. They gradually grew quiet. "There's something I need to tell you."

Everyone was focused on Barbara.

"This is the hardest decision I've had to make in a very long time. But I'm leaving with Wil to move to North Carolina."

Everyone's mouths dropped open but nothing came out.

"He built a house and he wants me there with him. I said yes to the new house and to his offer to marry him." A slow smile crept across her mouth as she pulled her hand out of her sweater pocket.

A collective gasp filled the room. Exquisite couldn't describe the brilliance of the diamond on Barbara's finger.

But the joy of everyone's announcement was tempered by the realization that Barbara was leaving them.

"We're happy for you and for Wil," Ann Marie said.

"But what are we going to do without you?" Stephanie asked, her voice thick.

Elizabeth couldn't speak.

Barbara looked into the eyes of each of her girlfriends. "It's because of each of you that I can leave," she began. "Through all the trials and drama that have gone on in our lives, you all always say it was me who saw us through it. But you all helped *me*. You helped me to be strong, to stand on my own two feet, to get back out into the world and find love again. I wanted to believe that I was so needed here that I could never go. What would everyone do without me?" She laughed. "Everyone will have a life, the lives we've all been working so hard to claim, that's what. I've finally found mine, because of my friends."

Tears of sadness, joy and acceptance drifted down their cheeks as they hugged and kissed and hugged some more.

Finally, Barbara stepped out of the circle. "I think we all deserve a toast." She went to the serving table and started handing out wineglasses, then filled each with sparkling cider.

They all raised their glasses and wiped at their eyes.

"To friendship, everlasting," Barbara said.

"Friendship," they chorused, and touched glasses.

"We have so many plans to make," Elizabeth sniffed. "Weddings, baby showers."

"House warmings," added Ann Marie.

"Going-away parties," said Stephanie turning to look at Barbara.

She grinned. "Hey, who says we can't franchise and open a *Pause for Men* in North Carolina?"

Their eyes widened with excitement and they all began talking at once.

Barbara looked at her friends and her heart was full. She might be moving away, but they would always be together in spirit and, from the sound of things, more adventures were surely on the way.

Can she surrender to love?

WORKING MAN

Favorite Arabesque author

MELANIE SCHUSTER

Funny and feisty Dakota Phillips has almost everything she wants. But her insecurities and independence have kept her from searching for the perfect man. Then she meets Nick—a self-made, take-charge mogul who makes Dakota feel beautiful, desirable and maybe a little too vulnerable. Dakota could easily move on... except for a little complication called love.

*Available the first week of July,
wherever books are sold.*

He's determined to become the
comeback kid...

THE
VERY
THOUGHT
of
YOU
ANGELA WEAVER

Drafted to hide a witness's daughter in a high-profile
murder case, Department of Justice operative
Miranda Tyler seeks the help of Caleb Blackfox,
who once betrayed her. Now Caleb is willing to do
whatever it takes to win back the girl who got away.

*Available the first week of July,
wherever books are sold.*

KIMANI™
ROMANCE

KPAW0260707

Almost paradise...

one gentle
KNIGHT

Part of The Knight Family Trilogy

WAYNE JORDAN

Barbados sugar plantation owner Shayne Knight fulfills
his fantasies in the arms of beautiful Carla Thompson.
Then he's called away, leaving Carla feeling abandoned.
But Carla goes home with more than memories...and
must return to paradise to find the father of her baby.

Available the first week of July,
wherever books are sold.

KIMANI™
ROMANCE

www.kimanipress.com

Forgiveness takes courage...

A MEASURE OF
Faith

MAXINE BILLINGS

With her loving husband, a beautiful home and two wonderful children, Lynnette Montgomery feels very blessed. But a sudden car accident starts a chain of events that tests her faith, and pulls to the forefront memories of a very painful childhood. At forty years of age, Lynnette comes to see that it takes a measure of faith to help one through the pains of life.

"An enlightening read with an endearing family theme."
—*Romantic Times BOOKreviews*
on *The Breaking Point*

Available the first week of July
wherever books are sold.

Celebrating life every step of the way.

YOU ONLY GET *Better*

New York Times bestselling author
CONNIE BRISCOE
and
Essence bestselling authors
LOLITA FILES
ANITA BUNKLEY

Three fortysomething women discover that life, men and everything else get better with age in this entertaining three-in-one anthology from three award-winning authors!

Available the first week of March wherever books are sold.

KIMANI PRESS™
www.kimanipress.com